# THINGS NOT
## TO DO

# THINGS NOT TO DO

STORIES BY

## JESSICA WESTHEAD

*Cormorant Books*

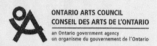

The publisher gratefully acknowledges the support of the Canada Council for the Arts
and the Ontario Arts Council for its publishing program. We acknowledge the
financial support of the Government of Canada through the Canada Book Fund (CBF)
for our publishing activities, and the Government of Ontario through the Ontario
Media Development Corporation, an agency of the Ontario Ministry of Culture,
and the Ontario Book Publishing Tax Credit Program.

LIBRARY AND ARCHIVES CANADA CATALOGUING IN PUBLICATION

Westhead, Jessica, 1974–
[Short stories. Selections]
Things not to do / Jessica Westhead.

Short stories.
Issued in print and electronic formats.
ISBN 978-1-77086-506-8 (softcover). — ISBN 978-1-77086-507-5 (HTML)

I. Title.

PS8645.E85A6 2017      C813'.6      C2017-904544-X
C2017-904545-8

Cover illustration: Julia Breckenreid
Interior text design: Tannice Goddard, bookstopress.com

Printed and bound in Canada.

CORMORANT BOOKS INC.
10 ST. MARY STREET, SUITE 615, TORONTO, ONTARIO, M4Y 1P9
www.cormorantbooks.com

*For Derek and Luisa*

# CONTENTS

Not Being Shy     1

The Lesson     26

Baby Can't You See?     42

A Little Story About Love     49

The Opener     58

Real Life     75

Gazebo Times     84

We Wish You Happiness, With All Your Friends Around     91

Dumpling Night     99

Things Not to Do     109

He Will Speak to Us     115

Everyone Here Is So Friendly     130

Empathize or Die     140

At Kimberly's Party     155

Prize     160

Puppybird     177

Flamingo                                        189
Escape to the Island                            202

Acknowledgements                                221
About the Author                                225

# THINGS NOT TO DO

# NOT BEING SHY

JUDY REMEMBERS HOW SHE used to get excited about the little things. Back in voice-acting college, for example, when she was out walking and stumbled upon the backyard dump with rusty appliances and stained mattresses and garbage everywhere, and then she saw the mama pig and her piglets emerge from a cardboard box, and it was like a miracle was taking place. Maybe to other people that scene would not have been so extraordinary — they might have thought, *Oh look, pigs.* They wouldn't have been totally blown away with wonder like Judy was, which is why she was described by her boyfriend at the time as "whimsical."

Judy has not felt whimsical for a while. Her most recent boyfriend, whose name is Jasper, was in the news last year because he'd constructed an elaborate underground chill-out room, furnished with a beer fridge and a TV and a beanbag chair, in a remote wooded section of a large public park. He used to always leave and not tell Judy where he was going, so after she read the article, she finally knew where he'd been spending most of this time.

He was home with her, though, the morning a city employee plummeted into the tunnel opening, which Jasper had concealed with mud and sticks and discarded fast-food packaging. The worker didn't report what he'd found right away. He later told his manager that he'd twisted his ankle really badly and was quite freaked overall by the whole discovery, so he needed to take a few hours to rest. His description of the mysterious burrow went viral, and by the end of the day, everybody knew that the fridge was stocked with boldly flavoured microbrews and an assortment of snack cakes, the TV got a bunch of channels, and the beanbag chair felt like a big, fluffy cloud.

The authorities assumed terrorists were involved, because why wouldn't they be, so there was a lot of fear circulating until Jasper came forward and explained to the police department that this was just a place for him to hang out, away from his girlfriend, and watch what he wanted to watch and eat what he wanted to eat and just enjoy himself with no strings. The male cops were like, "Oh yeah, we totally get that, no worries at all." The female cops were like, "How does your girlfriend feel about all of this?" The male cops rolled their eyes and said, "It doesn't matter what she thinks. That's the whole point."

Then Jasper started making tacos for a living, and the business took off because everybody wanted to buy a taco made by That Guy, the guy who needed to get away from his girlfriend so bad that he basically dug a hole in the ground where he could finally have a little peace.

And Judy really wanted to be happy for all of his success, but it was hard. It was pretty hard to get out of her own way and not feel sorry for herself over the whole situation, because she personally was not having success at her chosen career, which was voice acting. So far she had worked as a voice actor once, and then never again.

Meanwhile Jasper had started sleeping with Lisa, because she was gorgeous and could walk around on high heels like they were part of her body, like they were dainty, spiky gazelle hooves that could slice Judy wide open if she ever encountered Lisa in a forest — which would be weird, but then again, weird things happened all the time, especially in forests. And because, Jasper told Judy in his overly mellow explaining voice, Lisa actually listened to him for a change instead of just talking about how she wanted to make meaningful use of her wasted creative potential all the time. And besides that, Lisa supported him in what he wanted to accomplish with his life, which was to finally do the CN Tower EdgeWalk, which Judy had never let him do because she was too scared he would fall. But he wasn't going to fall, was the moral of the story that Judy had never understood. He was going to put on the protective suit and the safety harness and listen to the instructions and follow them and then when he was done having the biggest thrill of his entire existence, he was going to celebrate and go for beers. With Lisa.

But things are looking up for Judy, because the other night while sleeping in her bed all alone, she had a dream that took place in her old high school. The halls were empty and all the

classroom doors were closed. She kept opening them and finding her old teachers, but instead of being the age they were
when they taught Judy, they were newborn babies. And yet
they spoke in their regular voices and still knew lots of things
about math and science and English literature. A few of them
asked Judy what she was up to these days, and she shrugged and
said, "Oh, this and that." And then her geography teacher, who
had always been her favourite because she used to write reassuring, geography-related adages on the blackboard such as,
*Remember that here is not the only place*, shook a pastel-pink rattle
under Judy's nose. "Hey," she said, "remember, like the ancient
peoples who migrated across the Bering Land Bridge while
tracking large game herds, you've come a long way."

Judy woke up feeling valued and encouraged, and shortly
afterwards she had the idea to manufacture a doll and use her
specialized voice-acting skills to record a selection of phrases
that would be inspirational to shy children. Judy had been a shy
child herself, and maybe if she'd owned such a toy she would
have grown into a less timid adolescent who actually enjoyed
high school instead of hating every minute of it.

The uplifting phrases will go onto a computer chip and the
computer chip will go into the doll, so that when a shy kid
presses a button, or maybe squeezes the doll's hand for comfort
or companionship, they will hear Judy's soothing and melodic
vocalizations and instantly become self-assured.

Marketing is important, so she'll need a catchy slogan to get
people's attention. A call to arms for bashful children and their
caregivers, such as, *Unharness the more ebullient part of yourself*

*from deep down inside.* Or maybe something more straight to the point, like, *Freedom.*

Once her invention is available for purchase both online and in stores, Judy is sure the demand will be huge. She'll make tons of money, of course, but the tsunami of gratitude from millions of formerly shy souls, plus spin-off voice-acting work in major motion pictures, will be her true reward.

All she needs now is a factory to make the dolls and a studio to record her messages and an I.T. department to figure out how to put the messages on some chips and then how to put the chips in the dolls. Into their heads, maybe? Behind the mouth? Would there have to be a speaker somewhere? Judy still has a lot of questions, but as a no-longer-shy person — because hey, she *has* come a long way! — she is confident she'll find the answers.

JUDY IS NO FOOL, but there were definitely warning signs about her and Jasper's impending break-up that she failed to recognize at the time.

She was feeling mostly satisfied in the relationship, but was also going for a lot of walks and listening to a lot of 10,000 Maniacs and singing along in a voice that was full of outrage.

When winter was finally over, Judy started getting excited that all the snow was melting but Jasper didn't seem excited at all, which was weird for him because he had always been a big spring fan.

She could think back on those things now and smack herself in the forehead for not realizing what was going on, but that would be an act of self-hatred, and self-hatred is not what Judy is about. What she is about is owning a wallet shaped like a fish, which is a cute and quirky conversation starter that helps her instantly connect with other human beings.

The other day she was getting out her Visa card to pay for a box of white wine, and the liquor-store cashier remarked, "Hey, now that's a wacky wallet if I've ever seen one!" He went on to wink and ask, "Is it waterproof?" To which Judy replied, "No." Then she got the joke — *because fish swim in the water!* — and she bobbed her credit card up and down as if it were being gently manipulated by waves, and the cashier smiled but didn't full-on laugh. He rang in her wine and then she was on her way.

SO HERE COMES LISA all of a sudden, hanging around the taco stand all the time and turning the hot sauce bottles upside down and dripping sensuous habanero drips onto her fingers and licking them and squealing, "Ooh, that *burns!*" And Jasper's giving her free tacos and even naming a signature taco after her, like who even wants to eat something called The Lisa, because it brings to mind absolutely nothing.

Meanwhile, Judy was there as the official Taco Girl from the beginning, meaning her job was to wear short-shorts and high heels and a baby tee that said, *My Taco Is Your Taco*. Mostly the people who that advertising worked for were guys who would harass her. She'd be trying to direct them down the alleyway to where Jasper had set up the hibachi, and they'd be trying to corral her up against the wall. So she'd yell for Jasper to come and kick their asses, but he wouldn't hear her over the Beastie

Boys playing on his old boom box that he'd grabbed from his mom's house — also to entice patrons, but mostly the loud music just served to cover up her shouts for help. So she'd have to constantly explain to these gropey guys that she wasn't what was for sale, and they'd call her a whore, which was the exact opposite of what she'd just told them, and maybe they'd go and buy a taco but probably not.

It was either that, or people would ask her if she knew that annoying bitch the taco bro was dating, like was she a total psycho or what? Judy would say, "I'm the annoying bitch." They'd go, "Really? You're not that bad-looking." And they were giving her a compliment so she'd have to say thank you, or else her mother's voice would fill her brain and demand to know why she hadn't thanked the person who'd gone out of their way to say something nice. That would be worse.

After all that, was there a single item on the menu called The Judy? Nope.

She's going to air this grievance with Jasper the next time she sees him, which will be tomorrow, because that's when he'll be selling tacos at his very first outdoor community event. Judy is going to be there to cheer him on because that's the kind of supportive ex-girlfriend she is.

Even though he called her up earlier today and said, specifically, "Judy, please do not come to the Donkey Rescue Fair. I don't want you there and Lisa doesn't want you there and neither does her kid, who hasn't even met you but if she did, she would definitely not want you there. So please, please, please stay away."

So she's going. Also, Lisa has a kid?

THE NEXT DAY, JUDY buys some cotton candy and thinks to herself, *You might see one homeless donkey in your life if you're lucky. You might be out walking in a field, and whoa, what is that over there, is it a horse? Nope, it's a donkey.*

But right now Judy is surrounded by dozens of them. Except they are no longer homeless because they have been given sanctuary, which is part of Lisa's job — she goes out into the world and finds donkeys just wandering around, and shoots them with a tranquilizer gun and loads them onto a flatbed and brings them here, to the Donkey Rescue Farm, which is being called the Donkey Rescue Fair today because the other part of Lisa's job is to annually drum up funds for the animals' upkeep by renting a cotton-candy machine and a bouncy castle, and — this year — hiring her new boyfriend to sell tacos.

Of course there is a massive lineup in front of Jasper's truck — he is definitely the main attraction, which makes Judy wonder about the convenient timing of Lisa's hook-up with him — so Judy waits her turn patiently because what else is she supposed to do, yell and scream and pretend to be crazy and scare all the customers away? Which, yes, is something she did after he broke up with her, but nobody could blame her for that, because she was upset and distraught and definitely not in her right mind at the time, due to being overwhelmed by sadness.

But she's going to keep it together today because today is about the donkeys.

Jasper sees her at the back of the crowd and scowls. He mouths, "Fuck off."

She mouths back, "Where's Lisa? I haven't seen her any-where. And where's this kid I've heard so much about? Actually all I've heard is that she exists, which was pretty surprising. So what, all of a sudden you're Mr. Commitment and a respon-sible parental figure? Give me a break."

He shakes his head and points to his ears and does an overly violent shrug, then continues assembling meat and condi-ments and tortilla shells and wrapping everything in his new branded napkins. She's seen them floating around town — they say, *MyEX-ICAN MADE ME DO IT*. Which doesn't even make sense, but when she thinks about it now, she realizes it's sort of like he's named something after her, after all. So she steps out of line, still hungry but satisfied she got her basic point across.

JUDY HAS BEEN WORKING on her assertiveness. She recently came close to ending a toxic friendship that has historically and presently exerted a very negative influence on her self-esteem.

She and Annabelle have known each other for a long time. Back during high school, they had this ritual at least one night a week where they'd drink lemon gin mixed with Gatorade and then run around the neighbourhood and pee on people's gardens. It was this special, rebellious thing they did together, like they were blatantly disregarding social norms and risking potential humiliation in order to declare their unique sisterly love to the world. Although they never got caught, so it was only ever the two of them who knew that the mutual urination was going on.

The part that made squatting over flowers in the dark less

appealing for Judy was how good her friend looked doing it. She was like a sexy magazine ad for outdoor toilets, with her classic faded 501s coiled around her sleek, sun-kissed calves and ankles. And then there was chubby Judy, dribbling onto her shoes. But it was sort of like her better-dressed and more attractive friend was giving her permission, like, *Yeah, you can pull down your baggy pleated cords in front of me and reveal your puffy, white legs, I don't mind. It's cool, because we're friends and I won't judge you for not having a body that's as nice as my body. Look at us! We're peeing on a garden!*

Then Judy went to voice-acting college and learned new things and lost a few pounds, and met new people who she's not in touch with anymore but who at the time were fun and kind and interesting, and Annabelle was not with her because she'd gone somewhere else.

For two years, Judy felt as if the whole benevolent universe was opening up to her, like, *Hey, here I am, dive on in*. She drank Strongbow and played pinball and attended concerts and bought an oversized yellow leather jacket from a thrift shop. She experimented with different hair products because she had always used mousse, but maybe mousse was not the way to go. She wore army boots with skirts and asked random guys for shoulder massages, and they gave them to her.

A few weeks ago, Judy and Annabelle were having lunch, and Judy found herself remembering how the whole campus had sparkled like a sparkly playground, even the restrooms. She thought about how funny and poignant and raw the graffiti in those college stalls had been — what a slice of life! — and how she used to just sit there and read and be filled with optimism.

Annabelle was telling some sort of anecdote about how great she was and by extension how lacking in greatness Judy was, but in a highly indirect way so that Judy couldn't quite pinpoint why this story was causing her pain, and Judy tuned her out so she could focus on recalling all the good times she'd had with this friend, but also all the bad times.

After a while, Annabelle stopped talking and said, "Are you listening to me, or what?"

Judy sat up straighter. She said, "I think part of my problem is that when I'm around you, I still feel like your fat sidekick."

"Aww, you shouldn't feel that way." Her friend smiled and reached across the table to pat Judy's hand. "You're not my side-kick anymore."

JUDY FINDS LISA HAVING a cigarette outside the bouncy castle. She goes over and stands next to her.

"Fuck," says Lisa. "I thought Jasper told you not to come."

Judy peers through the murky window of the inflated fortress. There is a single tiny child jumping up and down inside. "That your kid in there?"

"Yep."

"She's cute."

"Thanks." Lisa blows some smoke in Judy's face.

Judy coughs. "What's her name?"

"Collins."

"Like Tom Collins?"

"Yep."

"Cool, those are good."

"Uh huh."

"Can I ask you a favour?"

"Are you serious?"

Judy takes a naked plastic baby out of her purse.

Lisa says, "Jesus."

"This is a prototype for a doll I'm going to make to help shy kids, but I have to do some market research first. I need to get feedback from some actual shy kids. Is Collins shy?"

"She's moody as hell, I can tell you that." Lisa takes a last haul off her cigarette and then crushes it underfoot. "She'll throw a fit if I don't give her the right colour of bendy straw and then she'll be all in my face wanting validation or whatever. The only book she ever wants me to read anymore is about this mother aardvark who tells her baby aardvark that she would love her even if she wasn't an aardvark. Like if she was another animal or something. It's a stupid story, but it's her favourite. She's only three, though, so you can't expect much. She's always saying weird shit too. The other day I'm listening to the news in the car and they're saying, 'A woman's body was found, blah blah blah,' and Collins says, 'Why did they have to find the woman's body? Can't she find it herself?' And I'm like, *Fuck, I have to tell her about death now, and probably rape and everything else.* But then she got distracted by a red truck she saw out the window, and she says, 'Mama, is that a fire truck?' And I say, 'No, it's just a red truck.' And she goes, 'Why is it red?' I said I had no idea. But I guess I'm going to have to give her the death talk and the rape talk at some point, right? I mean, it's coming. She can't live in a bubble or whatever. She's got to know about the world. And it's got to come from me."

Judy says, "What if there was a doll that could do it for you?"

"Fuck," says Lisa. "That would be amazing."

WHEN JUDY FIRST MET Jasper, he grabbed her hand like it was a big handful of candy that was being handed out for free.

That made her happy because her previous boyfriend had expected her to take a bus all the way to another city so he could see her one last time and make sure he definitely wasn't attracted to her anymore. And nope, he wasn't.

After he dumped her and before she rode the bus back home, Judy went into his bathroom and stood in front of the mirror for a long time trying to figure out exactly what was wrong with her. She'd lost weight since high school, so what else was there?

She cheered herself up by going out to dance clubs and listening to songs about forgetting all your troubles temporarily so you can cut loose and enjoy yourself for one crazy night at a dance club. Which was where a cute guy named Jasper said he was really glad to meet her but he was really drunk so she should probably do some shots with him.

And he didn't even know, until she told him, that she was a very talented person who had once worked in an extremely competitive creative field. And then when she told him, he didn't care, because it was in the past and he said all he cared about was the future, and the possibilities that would spread out before him like the view of Toronto he would someday have from the top of the CN Tower.

Judy said, "That's really high up." Jasper said, "Hey, don't limit me, okay?"

COLLINS ROCKS THE PLASTIC baby in her small arms and sings it a nonsense song about peanut butter being good and frogs being bad.

Judy says, "Do you like it, Collins?"

"It goes in my sandwich," the little girl coos, "but they are too sliiiimy!"

The two of them are sitting side by side on a hay bale. Judy has her pen poised over her notebook.

Lisa is off somewhere doing fair-related business because she said Judy seemed trustworthy enough to be alone with Collins if she wanted to ask her some research questions or whatever. Judy said she was flattered but maybe she should get Lisa's cell number just in case, and Lisa said don't worry about it, she'd get Judy's number from Jasper if she needed to get in touch.

"What do you think of the doll?" Judy asks Collins now. "I want your honest opinion."

"I love her," Collins whispers. "I love her more than dogs."

Judy frowns. "Did you say 'dogs' or 'frogs'?"

Collins kicks her legs against the hay bale and laughs uproariously. "Grass can't be yellow and a chair! That's funny."

"What if she could talk to you and say things to make you happy, plus teach you all about life? Would you like that?"

"Oh-oh." Collins drops the baby on the ground. "She fell down."

Judy's cellphone rings and she answers it. "Hello?"

Lisa says, "You guys having fun? Because Jasper's going on break so we're gonna go on break together. Eat something or whatever."

Collins climbs off the hay bale and lies next to the doll. She closes her eyes. "Put us in the donkey truck, Mama."

"Is she talking about the donkey truck again? I bring her with me one time and now she's scarred for life. I told her, 'I'm not killing them! They're going to wake up later!' But that's not how she remembers it. Take her for some ice cream if you're looking for something to do. There's a place across the road from the farm. She goes mental for it. It's funny to see. She'll do tricks if you want. Okay, I'll call you later."

Judy listens to the silence on the other line, then hangs up too. She closes her notebook.

Collins says, "All babies cry when they get born."

JUDY'S ONE AND ONLY voice-acting gig was an ad for a home security system.

It was a few years ago, but if somebody stopped her on the street today and asked her to recite the entire radio spot — which nobody ever would — she could do it word for word.

There was that time when she and her mother were out for dinner, and after they ordered their food, Judy started telling her mom that when she asked Annabelle what she thought of Jasper, Annabelle said he couldn't be trusted because he'd taken way longer than any of Judy's other boyfriends to check out Annabelle's breasts, which were much larger than Judy's breasts.

Their waiter suddenly ran back to their table and jabbed a finger at Judy. "I knew you sounded familiar. You're the Arma-Get-It-Done girl! Say one of the lines for me. Say the line about the really bad thing!"

"Oh my goodness," said Judy, quietly bursting with joy. "You've caught me off guard here."

"Ha!" He clapped his hands. "Look at you, being all context-ually punny. Now let's hear it."

Judy blushed, and grinned, and cleared her throat.

Judy's mother said, "You know, now that you're here I think I'd rather have the Greek dressing."

"Oh yikes," said the waiter, "I'd better get that into the computer pronto or the kitchen'll be super pissed off."

"That's all you used to do when you were little," said her mother when the waiter hurried away. "Just sit around doing weird voices. You never played with other children. I was so relieved when Annabelle came on the scene."

"Mom," said Judy, "Annabelle is a toxic friend. She makes me feel bad about myself. I don't think I should spend time with her anymore."

"Well," said her mother. "That would be a mistake."

Alone in her apartment that night, Judy sat in front of a mirror and said, "You know how you can be going about your daily business and an alarm goes off for no apparent reason? You're in the middle of grocery shopping, for instance, and there's the alarm, but there's no announcement about why it's going off and if there's actually danger somewhere. So you're waiting for someone in a position of authority to come along and reassure you or else tell you to evacuate and leave all your cherished personal belongings behind because they will only slow you down and you seriously need to run. But nobody comes. So you keep doing what you were doing previously, which was grabbing cereal, but meanwhile you're thinking, *Damn, that alarm is really loud. But okay, I guess it doesn't mean anything. Maybe they're testing the system. Systems get tested all the time, right? For sure.* Then you slowly start looking around for evidence that something might have gone horribly wrong with society and there's about to be mass anarchy with ordinary people tearing each other apart in the streets. Those clanging bells certainly sound like they're heralding doom. A few of your fellow shoppers seem to be shopping a bit faster, perhaps anxious to get home and ensure the safety of the family members and pets and priceless heirlooms that are important to them. Like you, they came here to pick up their second-favourite kind of cereal because it's on sale this week and it's normally very expensive cereal. And like you, they're wishing either the alarm would stop, or the Really Bad Thing would just hurry up and happen already."

Judy paused to smile at her reflection, and her reflection smiled back.

"With Arma-Get-It-Done, say goodbye to the annoying uncertainty of false alarms, and say hello to the Really Bad Thing. Because if you hear us, it's happening. Specifically, it's happening in the place where you live. But hey, at least you'll know for sure."

JUDY BUYS COLLINS SOME ice cream but doesn't ask her to do any tricks. They make their way over to Judy's little car, and Judy tells Collins she can sit in the front seat and finish her cone but only if she is very careful.

Judy buckles her in and leaves the radio off, and on their way to the forest she reflects that there is a special type of security that comes with having a family.

Not only do you have the shared sensation of loving and being loved in return, but you all have a common goal, which is to go forth into the world as a coherent unit. And if one of you were to say, "I'm a bit sad today," the others would rush to comfort you, and you'd feel better. Then you'd go out for dinner at a family-friendly restaurant and draw on the placemats and eat chicken fingers shaped like dinosaurs.

Of course, sharing the jubilation of being a parental figure with a committed partner and thereby achieving a true sense of belonging is not the only game in town. Maybe Judy could go to the Humane Society and take home a cat that would otherwise be euthanized. How fulfilling would that be? Totally fulfilling. She'd be saving a life! But then she'd have a cat, and a cat is something she has never wanted to have.

Then you've got parents like Lisa, who are the problem at the heart of everything.

Seriously, who calls their daughter Collins? It's not even a name. It's the less-namey part of an alcoholic drink. Though

Judy has to admit it suits the kid somehow. It's actually perfect for her, because she's plucky. She's a plucky kid.

WHEN JASPER BROKE UP with Judy, he said it was because of her Facebook pregnancy announcement.

She said, "But it was just a joke for April Fools' Day. I thought you'd think it was funny."

People had still fallen for it, though, which was the problem. They'd left comments such as, *Congratulations!* for her, and on Jasper's page they wrote stuff like, *Oh, shit.*

Jasper had texted her a series of question marks, and Judy knew she was in trouble. The thing was they hadn't even got to the point where they'd talked about having kids with each other, so she'd figured he'd know she was making it up. But he didn't.

After he packed up his things and left, Judy cried herself to sleep. But that night it was as if someone was looking out for her, because she was comforted by her favourite recurring dream, which she hadn't had since high school.

It was the one about the two old-fashioned gangsters who were polite in that gravelly, threatening way from the 1950s, so you instinctively knew you weren't supposed to cross them. They had broken into her childhood home and there was Judy, an innocent teenage girl in a flimsy nightgown. The second-in-command perverted gangster was eyeing her up and down, but the head gangster, who was a gentleman, told him to "Stay the fuck away from her, do you hear me?" Judy was not to be touched. So she felt protected, even though the head gangster had just shot her mother and father in the backs of their heads, execution-style.

She wept for a while for her murdered parents, but then the head gangster offered to make her some coffee and she felt better, because she was only fifteen and had never been allowed to drink it, and now there was a handsome adult criminal straight out of a black-and-white movie pouring her a huge, hot mug. She thanked him, and savoured it while he pistol-whipped his creepy partner in defence of her honour.

Then in walked Annabelle, looking sexy as usual, and she immediately started flirting her slutty face off like she always did. Judy sat there, waiting for the men to smile at her friend and take turns admiring her long, curly hair and perky little butt and then tell her all the disgusting things they wanted to do to her. But they didn't. They didn't even look at her. They only wanted Judy.

When Judy woke up, she felt invigorated by imaginary caffeine and filled with a sense of purpose. And even though she didn't know what that purpose was yet, it didn't matter, because it was something, and something was always better than nothing, wasn't it?

JUDY HAD NOT IMAGINED there would be so many trees. She had figured, how wooded could a park actually be? Pretty wooded, as it turns out.

Collins hugs the plastic baby to her chest and tells it not to worry.

"You can keep that one if you want," Judy tells her. "I got it at the dollar store and its face is kind of wonky. The real ones are going to be cuter."

"I think she's nice," says Collins.

Judy smiles, and reaches down to give the girl's tiny hand a squeeze.

"Whoa," says Collins, "this is deep grass."

"You seem like a good person," says Judy. "I'm sad to say that there will be people in your life who will be mean to you for no reason."

Collins cradles the baby doll and hums softly to it, and begins to skip.

Judy takes a cleansing breath deep into her diaphragm. "There will be other people in your life who will get lots of fame and adoration for nothing very special. They'll have tons of fans who'll do crazy things to show their devotion, but they won't deserve it, because they never even tried very hard. They just did something, and people liked it."

Collins says, "I'm still hungry."

"Collins, do you know what you want to be when you grow up?"

The little girl is quiet for a moment. Then she answers in a hushed, reverent tone, "Maybe the ocean."

Judy nods. "Like a person who works in the ocean? That's cool. Well, let's say you go to ocean-worker school, which is the opening chapter on the path to realizing your greatest aspiration, and your instructors tell you that you have a natural talent, so you feel encouraged. Then you go out into the world with your diploma and all your abilities, and you get your first job doing ocean work and you love it so much and you're so thrilled to actually be getting paid to do this thing that you love so dearly. But then for some reason you can't understand, nobody ever calls you again, and you never get another chance to work in the ocean and enjoy its numerous underwater treasures while feeling self-actualized and proud of yourself."

Collins looks up at Judy with wide, anxious eyes. "Crabs have claws that pinch us."

"Yes, they do." Judy takes the child's hand again, and holds on.

Collins says, "Tell me another story."

"Okay," says Judy.

They keep walking, and Judy tells Collins that back when she used to get lonely and wander the city trying to find where Jasper was hiding, before the headlines and the tacos and Lisa, when it was just the two of them, she would step off the sidewalk into any grove-like area she came across. She knew he was somewhere in the wilderness because he'd told her from the beginning that he was an outdoorsman, and she had said great, but secretly hoped he would never ask her to go camping with him because she hated camping. In the end it didn't matter, because he never did.

She would stand there amid the trees and look up at the sun filtering down through the branches, and feel the most at peace she had felt in a long time. And then she'd hear a twig crack somewhere and start to worry that an animal was sneaking up to attack her, so she'd get back on the sidewalk.

"I don't like animals," says Collins.

"Me neither," says Judy.

"Look!" Collins hops up and down. "Some mud!"

Judy's cellphone rings and she ignores it.

She had really thought they were going the right way, but now she's beginning to give up hope.

Then she sees the flowers. Just a few at first, scattered here and there. Judy quickens her pace and pulls Collins along with her. After several more steps they come to a clearing, and suddenly the blossoms are everywhere, covering the forest floor like a multicoloured shag carpet.

Collins scoops up a handful of cloth petals and sniffs them. She frowns. "I don't smell something."

There are wreaths too, and candles, and poker chips. Scotch bottles and beer bottles and stubbed-out cigars — every piece of trash an offering from Jasper's "man-cave disciples." She'd read about them in the paper last week.

Someone has even built an altar, and when Judy gets close enough she can see that the pillars are two giant piles of *Sports Illustrated* and *Men's Health*.

Perched on top are an old Atari joystick, a bong shaped like a cobra, the complete Blu-ray box sets of *Dirty Harry* and *The Fast and the Furious*, and an oversized novelty shot glass with the contours of a buxom lady's décolletage and the inscription, *Boobs are something that guys like*.

She glances at Collins, who is taking everything in, and wonders if it was a mistake to bring her here.

And then the little girl giggles and picks a miniature vanity licence plate off the ground. "Ooh, look, this came from a tiny vehicle!" She shows it to the googly-eyed plastic baby. "Maybe from a *doll* car!"

The plate reads, *Freedom*.

Judy says, "Isn't that funny."

She backs away, condom wrappers and peanut shells crackling underfoot, and shivers. She's not scared of falling because she knows Jasper's pit was filled in after it was discovered. But it'll be night soon, and she forgot to bring a flashlight.

Then Collins says, "I have to pee."

"Hmm." Judy peers at the darkening sky. "It might be a while until we get to a toilet."

But the little girl is already squatting by the shrine.

"Huh," says Judy. "You know, now that I think about it, I have to pee too."

"Do it!" shouts Collins. "It's fun!"

"Collins," says Judy, "I'm really glad we met each other."

Their united tinkling is musical, like gentle rain on leaves, and Judy closes her eyes and just listens for a moment.

Then there's a scuttling noise, and both girls jump and scream. A squirrel emerges from an empty pork-rind bag and scampers into the bushes.

Judy pulls her jeans back up shakily, heart hammering, and helps her ex-boyfriend's new girlfriend's daughter with her tiny, pink shorts.

"I want to go home," says Collins.

"Me too," says Judy.

Collins yawns and rubs her eyes, then lifts her arms. "Carry me."

Judy picks her up. Her cellphone rings again, and she switches it off.

Collins lays her head on Judy's shoulder and sighs.

"I just wanted to see it," Judy whispers to her. "But it's really not that big a deal."

# THE LESSON

LET'S START WITH WHAT the women are like. Because above all else, you need to prepare yourself for the women.

First off is the bride, and I'll give you a for-instance. Last week my fiancée went out with a big group of her friends, plus my mother and her mother and her two sisters, and one of her sisters' sisters-in-law, to pick out her dress. I said to her, "All those opinions? All those screeching voices telling you what to do? You are in for a world of hurt in that scenario."

She put her hand on my arm in that way she does — she thinks it's a soothing thing to do, but to me it's just patronizing — and said, "How about I handle my end of things the way I want to. You are in charge of the rental tuxedos and the music. That's all you have to do." Implying that my job — our job — is easy, that I only have to entertain an entire banquet hall full of inebriated wedding guests and give them the most ulti-mate night of their lives. When she says stuff like that and uses that tone with me, I get a pang diagonally above my heart that makes me think negative thoughts such as, *Maybe our impending marriage is a mistake.* It's as if she doesn't understand me at all.

Nah, but I'm just kidding. I love her more than anything. You got a girlfriend?

Then there are the bridesmaids. Actually, the bridesmaids aren't usually much of a hassle because they're too busy boo-hooing about how fat they look in their stupid matching dresses that they didn't get to pick out by themselves. They all end up hating the bride for dictating what they have to wear, but they distract themselves by talking about her behind her back and rubbing up against the best man. Even if he's married. Especially if he's married. There is something about two people publicly promising to love each other forever that brings out the lowest form of dogshit in everybody else.

Next up — okay, let's press the pause button for a minute because you seem a little distracted to me. You keep checking your phone, and meanwhile I'm imparting this information on a you-need-to-know basis. Think about it — if I was to walk away right now, leaving you and your limited skill set alone with all these people, they would eat you alive. And your fancy mobile device there would be like, "Oh shit, what do we do now?" Technology can only take you so far, and if you want to do this, you need to cultivate real-world knowledge. What's the Internet going to tell you that I don't already know? The answer is nothing. All right, so you're taking notes on your phone. That's good. If you're taking notes, that's fine. We can proceed.

As soon as the reception starts, you need to scan the crowd for troublemakers. See that woman over there, the one with the spiky hair and the feathers on her dress? What does she think she is, a bird or something? See how she can't sit still, how she's squirming in her chair? What? Aha, she's laying an egg, that's funny. Picking up on the bird motif, that's clever. You have to be quick on your feet in this business, I'm impressed.

But you need to listen very closely to me now. That is a woman who wants to dance, but she's the worst kind — she only wants to dance to her music. You can always spot her because she's straight out of the textbook. Not a real textbook, no. More like a textbook I made up in my mind. She'll be late thirties to early forties. She'll be drunk, and will get drunker. She'll have short hair, or medium-short hair, with sort of spiky bits or parts that flip out at the sides. She'll think she's cuter than she is. She'll believe she's going to charm you. And yeah, she'll be charming at first. Hell, she is cute. But not as cute as she thinks she is. She doesn't have much in the boob department. Her heels aren't as high as the other girls' heels.

Moving right along — and things move fast here, so you need to keep up — the first ingredient of a primo playlist is timing. You want to get the old people out dancing before everybody else because they're going to be gone before everybody else. Yes, right, gone in every sense of the word. Again with the comedy, I like it. But you need to focus on what I'm telling you. Ideally the old folks go home thinking — or saying, which is even better, but old people generally aren't big talkers so you settle for what you can get — *I had a good time. That was some kind of good time I had, yessir.*

Timing-wise also, you do not want to blow your best

material too fast. Look around — these guests are still eating dessert. If I played the new Beyoncé single right now, the majority of them are not getting up because they're neck-deep in chocolate mousse. You might get a couple of diehards on the dance floor, but that's it. Then you know what happens? Somebody's going to come up to you later in the evening and want that very same single again. Which puts you in the difficult position of saying you already played that song, but the guest wants to hear it again because now there are actually people dancing. And you're supposed to make the guests happy, so basically if you allow that chain of events to unfold, you're fucked.

If the bride has done her homework — and trust me, she'll do it — she will be intimately familiar with your style. She didn't just pick some random DJ off the street. She hired you because she wants you. Sure, she'll have her own songs lined up for the big dances, for the bride-and-groom, bride-and-father, groom-and-mother — what, you seriously think *he* picks that one? — and she might have a handful of do-not-plays, but otherwise the success or failure of her nuptial celebration is in your hands. And all brides want to believe that their party will go down in history as the best one ever, just like they're all under the grand delusion that stuffing themselves into satin and lace and sequins will magically transform them into supermodels on their special day.

When my fiancée was a little girl, she wanted to be a princess but her best friend was way prettier than she was. The boys at school fought each other over who got to walk her best friend home, and at one point so many boys were stealing so many flowers for this girl that people started staking out their gardens, hiding behind bushes with skipping ropes. That shit never goes away. Now my fiancée wears those fitness shoes that turn normal walking into more of an intense exercise. She says they're supposed to give her "fantastic legs, spectacularly lifted buns, and a stronger core." She's strolling around thinking she's getting this amazing workout, but in reality she's been duped by a clever ad in a women's magazine and her burning desire for spectacularly lifted buns.

I'm thinking to myself, how much can her buns possibly be lifted, anyway? I enjoy their current height fine already. Are these shoes going to strap her buns into a jet pack and zoom them into the stratosphere? What if her already high-enough buns ended up on her shoulders? That would just be bizarre.

The next playlist ingredient, which is also sort of the first, so you've got two first ingredients, is variety. Imagine this scenario: You go to Applebee's, you get seated comfortably in a booth, and you don't so much notice the music as you notice how it's enhancing your dining experience.

I want to meet the guy who puts those chain-restaurant mixes together. He's got to please everybody. Young, old, medium-young, medium-old, kids, babies. How does he make his selections? Does he conduct polls? How does he know what will appeal to the general population? We're all sitting there, tapping our toes in between bites and feeling excellent about the state of the world's affairs, and it's all thanks to one man. Pretty incredible. Of course, our job is actually harder in many respects. He's dealing strictly with ambience, whereas we have to set the mood and bring the noise.

Requests are a whole different animal. With teeth. Sharp ones, exactly. So okay, everybody likes what they like, right? And everybody's tastes are subjective. Objective? One of the two. You know what I mean.

A good DJ will always take requests, but you have to take them judiciously. Say Miss Feathers over there is begging for The Cure. Chicks like her always ask for the fucking Cure. You make her feel heard, like she has something to look forward to, but you make her wait for it. You want her to go nuts on the dance floor — and hopefully she can move — when "Friday I'm in Love" comes on. You want her shouting, "That's my song! He's playing my song!"

But there's a delicate balance. If you make her wait too long, she'll get pissed off and start badmouthing you to her friends, and possibly the wedding couple, about how you aren't taking requests and you were rude to her, blah blah blah. On the other hand, if it gets so she thinks she can just order whatever song she wants, whenever she wants it, then you have surrendered the reins and allowed the public to hijack your program. And that is a sorry situation that you one hundred per cent do not want to find yourself in.

It's all about wielding influence. People see the name of our company on a wedding invitation — because that's a clause in our contract, that our name has to appear there — and they immediately think, *Whoa, this is going to be a classy affair.* So you better make damn sure your shoelaces are tied and you're not wearing an inappropriate belt buckle. This one guy who used to work for us? He showed up at a reception wearing a belt buckle in the shape of a King Cobra, all coiled up to strike. It was pretty mind-blowing, but I was like, "What the fuck? This is a fucking wedding." Put that majestic eagle or howling wolf in a drawer for another day. This is an occasion for fragrant blossoms and shit floating in big vases with rainbow-coloured rocks at the bottom.

The next weapon in your arsenal is showmanship. Do you ever have that dream where you're supposed to give a presentation, and it's on something really boring, like sustainable development, but you've somehow devised a way to make it interesting? Like maybe you've got Powerpoints of *Herman* cartoons that relate to the subject? I love Herman, he's so fucking deadpan. But when you arrive, you realize you've left the cartoons at home, and all that's left are the boring parts, like about sharing food with poor people and all that? You don't know how you're going to get through this thing, and there's a huge audience, but you have to do it — it's your turn. That's the approach I take with DJing.

Dreams are crazy things, right? Last night I dreamed that I ran into the most popular guy from my high school, and I told him what I did for a living. Do you know what that means? It means I've made it. There's Shane Terpstra, just walking along, and I recognize him but he doesn't recognize me. I had to tell him, "Dude, it's me!" And he grabbed my lapels and pulled me in and said, "Looking good, man." The next thing he said was, "What are you doing with yourself these days?" His eyes were these crazy red slits, like a snake's eyes, that's the only thing that was weird about him. I said, "I'm a wedding DJ, Shane. I play music during the best moment of other people's lives." And he started to cry these gushy red tears of blood out of his crazy red slit snake eyes, it was pretty freaky, actually, and he was so ashamed by what he was doing with his own life that he wouldn't even tell me. Or maybe he was a vacuum-cleaner salesman, something shitty like that. Anyway, it was a good dream.

The bottom line is you have to look good. Everybody wants their wedding to be a YouTube sensation now, so they film the whole thing — not just the ceremony. I'm talking the receiving line, cocktails, dinner, dancing, all of it. In case the head table breaks into a surprise choreographed number, or the bartenders start juggling bottles, or the servers form a human pyramid and it turns out they're from the cast of Cirque du Soleil. Or the groom slaps a Velcro target on the bride's back and hands out Velcro bow-and-arrow sets to the ushers and tells them to "Fire at will, gentlemen." Or the maid of honour starts throwing cupcakes at her kids and screaming, "I can't enjoy comedy anymore because I pee when I laugh now, thanks to you idiots!" Or the twelve-year-old ring bearer drops acid for the first time and the next thing you know, he's naked with bleeding fork holes all over his skin. Nobody wants to miss that shit.

This means at any given moment you could be caught on camera and plastered across the Web for eternity, so you better look like you're standing there thinking, *I have been to a thousand weddings, but this one is truly special, and the love that these two people share is absolutely, positively going to last forever.*

*It is the purest love I have ever witnessed in all my many years as a wedding* DJ.

I have a few tricks up my sleeve to keep me in the moment. I transport myself to childhood and remember the smell of creosote from when I used to explore the train tracks by my parents' house, and I'd leave a penny out to get flattened. When I picked up that thin slice of metal afterwards I'd marvel at the weight of the train, how heavy it must have been, to do that to metal! But then occasionally the memory trick backfires and I'll think about the time Tito Bacchiochi — who we all called "Tits-o" but never to his face — held me down on the tracks, and Shane Terpstra and some other kids were standing around laughing and I could hear the engine rumbling in the distance. Tits-o jammed his elbow into my neck and said I'd be just like that old hobo who fell asleep drunk in the same spot and got run over. We'd all heard about it on the news. When they found him the next day, he was still alive but his left arm and leg were gone and he kept yelling, "Where are my cigarettes?" So actually certain memories are not the ideal ones to bring back, and they're a bad example of what I'm trying to illustrate here.

Oh yeah, there's plenty of perks. The free meals are pretty sweet. You get to take all sorts of free crap home. Our cupboards are full of shot glasses, mugs, vases, corkscrews, salt and pepper shakers, all with the bride and groom's names and the date they were married. Some of them also have a line about the love that was forged and strengthened that day — *Forever and always*, we have a few of those. *Two hearts united in one soul*, that kind of thing. Or, *It's not you, it's me*. No, haha, I'm just kidding about that one. That wouldn't have made sense at the time.

Back to what I was saying about requests. Last week I played in the Veils 'n' Cummerbunds Body Shocker Regional Finals, and I got a special Honourable Mention Crown for mass appeal. Not to say that I need an award to tell me what I'm worth. It was nice to finally get one, sure, but prizes don't mean anything in the overall scheme of things. I am widely considered to be the people's DJ. Which is of course exactly where I want to be, it's the biggest compliment you can get. That's why I'm here training you. I take on all the newbies because I know the ropes. I made the ropes, wove them out of whatever material goes into rope. String or whatever.

Anyway, at the contest, nobody had any requests for me, I was that good. I mean, they were all the DJs' wives and girlfriends so they knew the score. Except my fiancée was busy that night with wedding stuff, and that's fine. Priorities, right? In any case, I had them shaking everything God gave them, and then some. Ten DJs from the municipality, and out of all of them, I was the crowd pleaser. I knew what to play and when. I had my list. I had the songs lined up that went best together, and I had a full-on smile stuck to my face the whole time.

One part of the competition was for showcasing our MC skills. Because as a wedding DJ, sometimes you are called upon to MC, which I personally think is really sad. These people can't even dig up an uncle or brother-in-law or distant cousin who knows them decently well to tell some mushy anecdotes about them, so they have to hire a stranger to say those things? And yet that was the section where I got extra points. They said my MC work was so heartfelt, it was as if I had known this imaginary couple their entire lives. You want to know how I did that? It was because I was talking about my own relationship, and what we have together and all the romantic things we used to do together. When I talked about how the fake wedding couple met, for instance, I thought about when I first laid eyes on my fiancée. She started working in my local video store, and I literally had to rub my eyes when I saw her, she was that hot. Before I got up the guts to introduce myself, I used to drop little notes for her through the return slot, to capture her heart. It creeped her out at first but I guess it worked in the end, right?

Because I was thinking about all this, at one point I had real, actual tears in my eyes, and that's what the judges said put me over the edge. That's what won me a beautiful pair of Bose headphones fused onto a rhinestone tiara with flashing lights on it that needed a battery to work but nobody had a battery at the time, so I didn't get to see the full effect until I got home. Which, let me say, was totally fucking awesome.

I put my Honourable Mention Crown on the mantle over our fireplace, so my fiancée would see it when she got home. She said it was nice, and moved it into our bedroom closet because she said it would be safer there. Which made sense, I guess.

Did you see what just happened there? How Miss Feathers sidled over to ever so casually peruse our binders? She'll be back. At first she'll be all sweet. She'll act like she's your buddy, like she can read your mind, like you and her are a team.

But you are the one with the power. You've got all these partygoers waiting on you to press Play. All these couples staring into each other's eyes and secretly comparing their own relationship to the bride and groom's. *Why doesn't he put his arm around me like that? Why doesn't she look at me like that? Why doesn't he bring me flowers anymore? I thought we were more compatible. I thought we'd be having way more sex. Isn't he supposed to love all of me, all the time? Why didn't she say yes right away? Why did she have to stand there and think about it for thirty fucking seconds? Fuck this, I'm going out for a smoke and I'm never coming back.*

But then you bring them back, because your music is so fucking good, it's irresistible to their jaded ears.

What you need to do with women like Miss Feathers is you need to shut them down. Pronto. Otherwise they'll keep coming back for more. So you grant her the first one or two tunes she asks for, and then nothing after that. Trust me on this one, or she'll be leaning over your list at one a.m., breathing hard through her nose and going, "What's the name of that famous Bon Jovi song? The one everyone likes to dance to?" She secretly thinks she could do your job, better than you, even. She likes to think she's doing you a favour by telling you what music people want to hear. She thinks she has the finger on the pulse of humanity, but she doesn't know shit.

It's like how my fiancée wanted me to bring the phone book back into vogue. Like bringing sexy back, but with the phone book. "Look," she said, "it's got all these pages, with everything you could ever want. There's important services and not-so-important ones. If you have a need, you pick up this phone book and it will find a way to satisfy that need." Unlike our relationship, is what she meant to say, under all her rampant phone-book glorification.

And here's the crucial part of the exchange. She asked me, "Are you advertising your DJ services in the phone book? Because if not, you should be."

I know you're going to say, "Hey, chill out, she was only trying to help." But if you pay attention, I think you'll come out on my side of the fence on this.

I said, "Nobody uses the phone book anymore. It's an antiquated medium."

She said, "The past is coming back. Everything old is new again. People want retro." And at that point she suggested I look up "satisfy" in the phone book and see what they had to say. "They" as in the phone-book people. Who could read our minds, apparently.

She told me then that her deepest desire was for me to be the man she first met at the video store and later kissed in line at the go-kart track, who had hovered his hand over her back, reiki-style, or shiatsu or whatever, in any case, without actually touching, and with one twitch of his fingers — fingers that now only select songs for strangers to dance to — SPRING! her bra would magically come undone, and she would be standing there in awe of this man who had enticed her breasts to jump free of their coverings. Then she was next in line and had to ride a go-kart around and around the track with zero chest support. And she had never felt so free and alive in her life.

Do you know that in some cultures, women are treated like goddesses, but in others, they're treated like slaves? And there's no telling in some of those countries which way it's going to go. My point being, in some parts of the globe, women have to watch themselves.

Meanwhile, here in the Western hemisphere, you get a woman in her thirties or forties who thinks she's still in her twenties and she wears a dress with fucking feathers on it, to a wedding, and she thinks she's ten different kinds of hot but she's barely even one, if that. And we can ogle her legs and ass and tiny tits all we want, and she doesn't mind it. She likes the attention. And it doesn't occur to her to worry about the ogling because she believes she's surrounded by this impenetrable force field. But she's not. Because it would be so easy to break that thin shell, just press my finger against her little bubble and pop it all over her face.

What? Oh, I don't know. I'm just using her as an example. I could say the same for any of the women here. The bride, even. But probably not the bride, since she's got her big, tall, new husband with her this evening. After tonight, though, who knows?

Miss Feathers is an interesting specimen, let's call her. Not exotic. No. I wouldn't go that far. She's a smoker, for one thing, which is disgusting. See, there she goes again, out for another puff session.

And if I were to follow her, say, just as a for-instance, walk out there and introduce myself — as in my name, because she's already acquainted with my face — and maybe I'd cup my hands around her mouth, keep her lighter flame safe from the cold wind. Or else I'd let her fend for herself, depending on my mood.

I only want to talk to her, really. Ask her a few questions, see what makes her tick. I want to say to her, "Don't you think I know what I'm doing up there? Don't you think I've trained, gone to school for this? I have an actual framed diploma from an accredited institute that I happen to be very proud of. This is my career. And you think you know better than me what people like? What women like? You have your own ideas about how things should go? How about I show you how they should go, right now. How about I convince you, and maybe the next time you'll think twice about second-guessing every decision I make, about micro-managing every tiny little detail." And more words to that effect.

People need to be taught. They need to realize how the world works, and that there are professionals in their fields and chosen vocations. And professionalism needs to be respected.

You want to know how to be a great wedding DJ? You want to know the secrets? I'll tell you. You go to bed late and you get up early. There are no secrets. There's only you and me, right here and right now, on this dance floor.

And Miss Feathers, of course. There's always a Miss Feathers. Maybe she and I can arrive at an understanding together out there in the cold, quiet night while you carry on in here where it's warm and loud, sticking close to my list but maybe adding in a bit of your own variation, just a bit. You have to cut your teeth some time, right?

Worse comes to worse and I don't come back in for a while, you know how to keep the party going. The knowledge is yours now. And you've got all those notes you've been taking.

Yeah, sure, you can go to the bathroom first. That's probably a good idea.

# BABY CAN'T YOU SEE?

DARLENE MET KYLE AT a rave. Actually they met online. But they tell everybody they met at a rave, and then Kyle shouts, "She wanted my glowstick!" It's because of that joke, that's why they tell the rave story. Kyle is a joker.

For their first date they went to a noodle restaurant, which Darlene suggested, and Kyle said what made you pick this place, is it special or something. She said due to that thing he wrote in his profile about loving hot sauce, and he said, "Why do you love noodles so much?" She said, "Well, I guess because they're comforting," and he said, "Some people think comfort is a good thing, but I'm not one of them. I need to be sky-diving. I need to be plummeting to Earth at a thousand miles an hour, without you there on the ground holding a large, industrial-strength net to catch me."

Kyle values authenticity and would sell his dog for Sriracha. Just kidding, he doesn't have a dog! But he wishes he did.

Darlene's job keeps her busy. She works at a bank and has

no regrets. She once read on a greeting card her friend Melanie gave her that gratitude is a journey, and that the people you thank along the way become your fellow travellers. Darlene is grateful for her life. She is grateful for all the good things in it. She was grateful for the card when she received it. There was an absolutely breathtaking sunset scene on the front, which she briefly considered framing but then reconsidered. Darlene also has a small satin pillow hanging on the doorknob of her bathroom. It's shaped like a heart and reads, *I'd rather be in Paris*. She has never been to Paris, but she can relate. The pillow was another gift from Melanie, who always pays too much for things, or so she says.

Melanie lives alone. One night, she eats a shrimp ring and watches a documentary on the homeless population. She thinks, *Those people, their faces are so dirty but their eyes are full of hope. Plus anger.* She double-checks that her door is locked before she goes to bed. The documentary was depressing but the shrimp were delicious. They were jumbos.

Kyle used to have a wife. He has a recurring dream where he is still married and a massive, lethal cyclone is coming straight for him. He's at his office but is alone because all of his co-workers left early when they saw the storm warning on social media, which Kyle missed because he is not the kind of employee to go on social media when he is supposed to be working. And now he is smack in the path of an apocalyptic funnel cloud, and his wife is far away and out of cellular range. The action freezes like in a movie, and he utters one very powerful word: "STOP." But the tornado blasts through the glass anyway, and he falls to the ground and remembers how he and his wife discussed having a special designated meeting place in the event of a natural disaster, but they couldn't agree on where.

Melanie got together with her first boyfriend, whose name was Jordan but his friends called him Jordy, at a pool party at his parents' house when they were in high school. The parents were away and that was a good thing because the whole point of the party was that Jordan had put a fish in the pool. It was a big fish that he'd caught in a lake. Everybody was like, "Can it survive, though? In the chlorine?" The answer was no. The fish had beautiful shimmery grey and brown scales. It was gliding around the pool, but very slowly. The girls were screaming, "It's going to bite me, it's going to bite me!" The guys were throwing quarters at it and taking bets on when it was going to die. Jordan asked Melanie out at the exact point when the fish stopped swimming and started to float.

Darlene's favourite flavour is cherry, which is kind of boring but also kind of sexy. There was that party that she and Kyle went to. All the successful match-ups from their dating site were invited and the theme was Convenience, and guests were encouraged to hook their drinks onto their necks with a pipe cleaner device rigged with a straw. Darlene was sucking on something red — because, cherry! — and Kyle said it looked like mercury rising, like is it hot in here or what. And the various other couples around them appeared to be thinking, *Hmm, just look at the harmony between those two.*

Melanie slept with Kyle at one point, although she told Darlene it was him that initiated it, not her. Whereas he said it was Melanie's fault. But in the end it came out that it was actually mutual.

Kyle prefers the slight variation of his recurring dream, in which he is working at a juice bar making smoothies. He's pretty sure that part of the dream comes from how he enjoys whipping up smoothies at home, and they're so tasty that he often thinks he should be getting paid for his talent. Before the tornado hits, a satisfied customer is saying, "Your smoothies are amazing." Kyle winks. "The key is frozen bananas. They give it the ice-cream mouthfeel. Always use frozen bananas as your base and you can't go wrong." Then boom.

Darlene is compassionate and thinks of other people, but she also thinks of herself and that's okay, because only door-mats think of other people and never themselves, which means in reality they're bottling up their emotions and will someday explode all over an innocent bystander who says or does something slightly the wrong way. Such as the waitress at the Timmy Ka-Chingo's where Kyle and Melanie took Darlene to explain about the them-sleeping-together situation, who certainly waited a long time to come over and ask what the three of them would like to eat. And when she eventually did ask, maybe Darlene was a bit rude to her, which the waitress did not deserve. The young woman in her skimpy, corporate-mandated ensemble had even made a nice observation by saying, "Wow, that's a really beautiful sunset on that card, look at those gorgeous swirly pinks and oranges." So in that example, Darlene's unkind outburst definitely did not make Darlene feel any better. It made her feel worse.

Kyle is afraid of being badly hurt or killed by an extreme weather event caused by climate change. When he visits his parents, he feels safer. Their presence calls to mind his generally carefree childhood and therefore is like a soothing lotion of pleasant bygone years when global warming was not in the news. But then he thinks about them dying, possibly at the hands of a tornado but probably just from old age, and he feels like a little kid who has become lost in a mall. Which happened to him once, and his parents still tease him about it to this day.

Melanie is aware of the possibility that somewhere, a desperately unhappy person resents her happiness and wants to destroy it. She lies awake at night waiting for the sound of a window being smashed, clomping footsteps stopping outside her bedroom door. Probably no knock. The idea of a sorrowful, murderous lunatic home-invading her apartment is not so far-fetched because sometimes Melanie will be out somewhere in public, minding her own business, and a crazy person will come and sit nearby and eat a sandwich and stare at her.

Darlene was recently in a public restroom at a large chain restaurant that did not have toilet paper in any of the stalls. What the fuck was that about? She went from stall to stall checking for toilet paper, and there was none. Two early-twenty-somethings in Timmy Ka-Chingo's signature crisp, white shirts, black short-shorts, and playfully dangling bronze medallions came in and lit up cigarettes by the sinks. One of them said to the other, "You know, like, the adults? They act so concerned about the planet and shit. My mom buys the free-range eggs, like from the free-range chickens? But they were born into captivity, right, so they don't even know." The second girl jumped up and down, causing her medallion to jingle. "Yeah, free range! My mom buys those too. They taste so good." The first girl nodded. "Yeah. But then we're the ones — because the adults are totally going to die before us — so we're the ones who have to live with it, and deal with the Earth all decaying and shit." Darlene thought, *This is a large establishment in which the servers wear expensive-looking uniforms and there should be toilet paper in here.* The second girl smiled at her and said, "Oh my God, that sunset was so pretty, right?" and Darlene felt bad for not recognizing her waitress, who looked the same as all the other waitresses, but still. "It was," she said, and she smiled back at the young woman and tore off a long piece of rough paper towel.

"Gary," Kyle's mother says in front of him, to his father, "remember when poor Kyle got lost in the mall, and we finally found him in that gadget store that sold the electronic pets, and he was crying so hard we couldn't understand what he was saying?" And his father slaps his knee: "Hahaha, yes, poor little guy. He threw up too, didn't he, from all the distress?" Kyle had stopped to pet a robotic dog that was red and white and made a continuous "Yip, yip, yip" noise. Its tail wagged when he ran his small hand over its smooth body. It had no fur but that was okay, he would love it anyway. It was the cutest robotic dog he had ever seen. And then he looked up and his parents were gone.

Melanie didn't really go out with Jordan in high school. She just fell in love with him that day at Woolco, when he was riding a skid full of dairy products and pretending it was a giant skateboard. He rolled past Ladies' Clothing where she was folding sweaters, and sang "Two Princes" by the Spin Doctors like it was meant for her. Realistically it was probably meant for Darlene in Towels, but it seemed as if it could be for her, Melanie in Ladies' Clothing. Because Jordan was looking at her when he was singing it, pushing that yogurt-and cheese-laden skid along with one of his powerful legs, with his curly dark hair and cute squinty eyes, and she pictured them doing fun and wacky things together such as announcing their love over the Woolco P.A. system. They had the code to be able to do that.

At the bank, people are always coming around and asking for money for grieving co-workers. If Darlene knows who they are, she will sign the card and contribute ten dollars for the funeral wreath, or sometimes it's a gift certificate for Timmy Ka-Chingo's, which she regularly reflects is the last place she'd want to go if she lost a loved one, with those goofy names they have for increasing the size of your drink, like "Ka-Chingo It Up!" The food is decent but the atmosphere is overly exuberant, and she didn't know who had decided that was the best restaurant for the company's saddest employees, but then she heard that the CEO's niece works there. So, aha. Anyway, ten dollars is a lot of money. If Darlene is told the name of the grieving person and it doesn't ring a·bell, she will sign the card but that's it. She has to draw the line somewhere.

# A LITTLE STORY ABOUT LOVE

STAN AND CATHY WERE going to watch a movie where lots of sex happened, and it was going to be a sexy movie. And even though they were both uncomfortably full of sexy French food, they were going to watch this movie and it would give them sexy ideas.

And maybe by the end of the movie, after they had completely digested everything, they would take off each other's fancy-restaurant clothes, or maybe they'd just take off their own clothes to save time, since they were more innately knowledgeable about how their own various buckles and clasps and artfully concealed zippers operated.

Either way, they agreed that it had been a good idea not to change right away when they got home, into their oversized and gently stained T-shirts and stretchy sweatpants, because at some point the fancy clothes would have to come off, somewhere between after the sexy dinner and during the sexy movie and before bedtime.

So maybe while they were both undressed — at least partially though probably not one hundred per cent, because what kind of person changes into different underwear for bed? — maybe when they saw patches of each other's bare skin, following all that sexy food, and then after being influenced by the sexy movie, then maybe something might happen.

The whole night, after all, had been about romance from the start. That was why they'd gone to the French restaurant that they'd read about in the paper as being a top spot for romance. It was, in fact, rated among the Top Ten Most Romantic Spots in the city, and after being so named, it would surely have been totally packed on Valentine's Day. Which was why they'd decided, mutually, to wait until a week later to go there for dinner — better to allow the amorous crowds to disperse, which apparently they did — and also because they had a coupon, and it didn't start working until then.

To Stan and Cathy's intense delight, they discovered that even without the coupon the place was reasonably priced, no question about it. For half-decent French-style cookery in the city, the prices were excellent. The service was excellent too, at least until Stan produced the coupon at the completion of the meal and the waiter with a French accent pronounced it "kweepon." At that point it didn't really matter anyway because they were done eating, so it wasn't as if there would have been any repercussions, such as the waiter spitting on their food out of spite. But still, the "kweepon" bit was pretty patronizing, and snooty in the way that only French-sounding people can be snooty.

Up until then, Stan and Cathy had been having a great time.

And even though Cathy had specified that they only wanted tap water to drink, and they both passed on dessert — because they were already so full! — that was okay, the tap water was poured for them out of a charming glass pitcher and it even had pieces of fruit floating in it. That was a nice touch.

But ultimately the coupon, or rather, the waiter's reaction to it, had basically spoiled the whole experience. Stan and Cathy went home feeling cheap — but not cheap in a good way, the way that would have made them feel like flinging off all of their clothes and watching a sexy movie in the nude, or even skipping the movie altogether and simply falling upon one another, revelling in the nuances and peaks and valleys of each other's unique bodies, even though those bodies were dangerously packed with cream and butter and fleur de sel on everything, and multiple baguettes and foie gras and bisque and *beaucoup de* wine, and mussels bathed in even more wine, and decorative haystacks of frites, and more cream and butter and various sauces made from both, all of it curdling into unpleasantness once it came into contact with the bitter ire of their snooty French coupon-disdaining waiter.

So what they did was, once they got home, they remained in their clothes. They did, however, remove their socks, and they unfastened their most constrictive buttons and sat very close together on the couch. And they observed the movie very closely. Afterwards the air was bulging with sexy expectation. It was too much, though, all of it. Ultimately what Stan and Cathy most desired was a generous handful of minty antacids and the chance to close their eyes.

But when they allowed their exhausted lashes to lower, they were treated to beguiling versions of each other, playing like a second, secret movie on the insides of their eyelids, which the other person didn't know they had access to. But they did, and it rendered them much more attractive than either of them felt, being so crammed with French delicacies and battered by French indignation.

Stan and Cathy went to bed and indulged themselves in the soft folds of their sumptuous duvet, and they each had a dream wherein they had extravagant, fulfilling, and creamy sex for what seemed like hours, but was in fact only the time it takes an average person to brush an average set of teeth.

BEFORE CATHY MET STAN, she felt like a pizza.

Before Stan met Cathy, he felt like a stone.

This is the story of those feelings, in more detail.

On a seat in a bus sat a pizza. It was left there. Who would leave a pizza? But someone did. We're talking a whole, entire pizza, not just a slice.

Beneath the left front tire of the bus was a stone. Everyone leaves stones behind. There's not even a question in people's minds — sharp or smooth or large or small, it's "Goodbye, stone."

Back inside the bus, which was locked up until morning, the pizza had cooled to the same temperature as the air, which was neither hot nor cold.

The air outside the bus was chillier, but the stone didn't care. The stone didn't care about anything.

The pizza was a Hawaiian pizza, with ham and pineapple chunks. Hawaiian was one of the more exciting flavours available on the menu from the restaurant where the pizza was made, but the cheese was harder now than when the pizza was freshly baked. The pizza didn't notice the difference.

Under the other wheels of the bus there were other stones, which were pretty much indistinguishable from the stone under the left front tire. Someone who was not looking very hard would just lump them all together into one big category labelled "stones."

The pizza was sad.

The stone was sad.

Apart from their relatively decent childhoods, that was how it was for Stan and Cathy, until they were introduced to each other by mutual friends who were getting tired of hearing the pizza and stone analogies all the time.

AFTER A WHILE, STAN and Cathy decided to get married.

Not too long after that decision, they watched a lady magician flip up a card in what she clearly believed was a mysterious and triumphant way, but which in truth was just completely lacking in magic aptitude.

The card was a queen.

Cathy told her, "My card was a king."

"Well," said the lady magician, "at least they're both royalty!"

Cathy adjusted her tiara, which had rhinestones on it. She thought, *This magician is not the magician I was promised.* She was told to expect a sorcerer. She was expecting a wizard with a wizard's robe and a pointy hat.

The budget illusionist shouted, "Again!" and Cathy and her fiancé Stan focused their mental energies as they had been instructed to do.

Stan gripped Cathy's hand and thought that this was the main problem with the magician's approach right there. There were two different people picturing two potentially different cards, so how was this trickster supposed to guess what card was being visualized? It was impossible. He was beginning to regret hiring her for his and Cathy's engagement party, which was tomorrow. He was starting to have some serious regrets in that department.

The conjurer closed her eyes and shuffled the deck, which Cathy had to admit was slightly impressive, and then held up the six of diamonds. "Anybody?"

Stan and Cathy shook their heads.

The magician said, "I'm going to release the dove now."

Stan glanced up. The ceiling in their apartment was very low.

Fortunately, there was no actual bird. It was a facsimile made out of pipe cleaners and some Kleenex glued together, with raisins for eyes.

Cathy thought, *I love Stan*.

Stan thought, *I love Cathy*.


CATHY HAD ALWAYS DREAMED of nautical-themed nuptials.

Because Stan loved Cathy, his original notion was to fill the reception hall with water and to serve the hors d'oeuvres from an inflatable raft.

The difficulty came when the two of them worked out the

seating plan, and realized that between Stan's Aunt Phyllis's dead fisherman husband and the flower girl's life-threatening mollusc allergy, neither the elegantly mysterious and quite appealingly priced "Ghostly Mariner" chair covers nor the clam centrepieces would be feasible.

They scrapped the raft idea and the water too, and opted for a seafoam motif for the bridesmaids' gowns and life jackets for the groomsmen. Stan and Cathy would wear water wings and snorkelling gear during their vows.

They rented a dunk tank and decided to distribute fishing lures as sharp and dangerous favours — to everyone but Aunt Phyllis, who would get candied almonds. A few of the hooks might end up embedded in the cheeks of some of the slower-witted guests, but that was a risk they were willing to take.

Dinner would be a choice of chicken or beef. They didn't know any vegetarians, and frankly didn't care to.

ON THEIR WEDDING DAY, Stan and Cathy stood up in front of their assembled family and friends and regretted the water wings decision a little bit, because their arms stuck out awkwardly. But otherwise they were just really happy to be there.

The officiant talked, and Cathy thought about Stan. When she first met him, he felt familiar and exciting all at once, like riding her tricycle down the somewhat sloped part of the street she grew up on. Her snorkel mask fogged up with the memory.

Stan listened to the officiant using the word "helpmate," and was glad that Cathy's veil wasn't the kind that obscured her face and that her features were still mostly visible behind her diving mask because A) he loved to look at her, and B) now he didn't have to worry about lifting the veil and discovering that she had a horrifying zombie face underneath.

The officiant asked them the usual marriage-related questions.

Stan and Cathy had to remove their mouthpieces to say, "I do." They were left with deep rims circling their mouths.

The officiant said, "That's that, then."

They kissed. Everyone cheered.

Stan and Cathy had their photographs taken. They ate their dinner. They enjoyed their party.

The night got darker, and the guests went home.


STAN AND CATHY WENT to a hotel. Their suite had two bathrooms, and what was even crazier was, there was a telephone in both of them.

They each went into a bathroom and sat on a toilet. Stan called up Cathy, and then Cathy called up Stan.

What else is there to say in this type of situation? Basically just observations about what was around them: a sink, some small soaps, a bathtub with showering capabilities, some small shampoo bottles. Towels of varying sizes.

They hung up. They did whatever it was they had gone into the bathrooms to do in the first place.

They explored the rest of the suite. There was a kitchenette! With cupboards!

The cupboards were empty.

Stan yawned.

Cathy said, "I'm pretty tired too."

They got into bed. The bed was extremely soft. And yet supportive. Yielding, and yet firm where it needed to be. Could a bed undulate? The evidence pointed to yes. They took turns admiring the mattress topper, which according to the pamphlet was designed "to simulate a marshmallow-like effect." They both agreed that was no exaggeration.

They fell asleep.

THE NEXT MORNING, STAN was hungry, but there was no food. He wondered about ordering room service, but then remembered there was a family brunch to attend. Stan did not want to attend the family brunch, but at least maybe there would be peameal bacon there.

They got dressed.

Cathy hoped there would be balloons at the brunch, but when they arrived, there were not so many balloons. Actually, none. Just Stan and Cathy's relatives and some coffee and juice and a few trays of assorted muffins.

She sat next to her new husband in her parents' living room, on the flower-patterned sofa — the one she'd always hated because when she was a child, the flowers had looked like disapproving faces — and remembered all the balloons at their reception.

*We should've filled them with water*, she thought.

But of course it was too late for that now.

# THE OPENER

SHAWNA'S HUSBAND IS IN a band.

His band is not the type of band that people pay lots of money to see perform in large arenas. But his band does perform in large arenas. Because people pay to hear the headliner, and Shawna's husband's band gets to go first.

Last night, they were doing the one about the gravedigger who awkwardly comforts the sad widow who's weeping by her husband's grave, when suddenly a miraculous talking rat scurries over and convinces the widow that she doesn't need to mourn for her dead husband anymore because he never actually loved her to begin with. And the wife says she's not really surprised because whenever her husband kissed her, she never felt anything major. Then the gravedigger gallantly offers to dig up her husband so she can spit on his corpse or kick it or whatever, and she says no thanks, that's not necessary. But she's overcome by emotion and starts kissing the gravedigger, and the gravedigger kisses her back. Then she reflects, sadly, that it's still not the type of kiss she's been waiting for her whole life.

Which is Shawna's favourite song because it's so heart-breaking but also has that element of dark edginess, so she figured it would be a good one to get a video of. And when she panned over the audience, they were rocking out, though not as much as they probably expected to rock out for the headliner, who they were actually there to see.

She'd uploaded the footage to the band's Facebook page that morning, and Danny had watched it three times. He said to her, "Babe, you're a star." And she said, "No, babe, *you're* the star." And he said, "Yeah, I guess that's true. But you're a star wife."

She figured he'd want to have sex after that, but he didn't. It was sweet of him to compliment her, though, and understand-able that he wanted to clarify himself as well. Because obviously words are important to him, because he's a songwriter.

The headliner is Ellison. That's the name of the singer and also the name of the band. Shawna thinks that's pretty con-ceited. It's not even "Ellison and the Other Guys" or something more inclusive like that. But to Ellison, Shawna is just the wife of the lead singer of the opening band, so she keeps her mouth shut about it.

Shawna's husband's band is called The Cheat-o's. He thinks the name is clever because it also sounds like the popular cheese-flavoured snack food. But Shawna has never liked it because of the not-very-veiled implication that the band members have no problem with people maybe thinking they have affairs on their wives. She explained that to Danny when he first thought it up, and he said to her, "Come on. It's veiled."

Shawna is in charge of The Cheat-o's Facebook page. At first Danny didn't think the band needed a Facebook page, but Shawna explained that the good thing about being the opener was all the unsuspecting people who would discover the immense talent of his band for the first time. And maybe some of those people would search for his band on the Internet afterwards, and probably at first they'd spell the stupid name wrong and end up on the Frito-Lay website and be confused, but if they were determined, they'd eventually find The Cheat-o's Facebook page and maybe they'd click the Like button. Or maybe they wouldn't. But at least that's something to measure, which is called analytics. Danny says he doesn't care about analytics, but Shawna keeps telling him analytics are important.

The thing about Ellison is, her body is so tiny but her hair is so big, which makes her body look even tinier. Shawna has thought about trying this trick herself sometimes, but unfortunately she was not blessed with the kind of hair that has the capacity to get as big as Ellison's. Shawna's hairdresser says she has a lot of it, but it's fine hair, which is just a nicer way of saying limp.

Shawna used to worry about her weight but she doesn't so much anymore. Now that she's in her late thirties, she's reached this great phase of her life where she feels comfortable with her own body.

Although she had a bit of a setback when she visited her parents last weekend. She dropped in when The Cheat-o's did a show in their city — Danny really wanted to visit too but he couldn't because he had to practise and then relax after practising — and when she was there, she found a box of diaries from her youth. She read some of them. Now she thinks that was a mistake.

She was hanging up an outfit in her childhood closet, which still has most of her old clothes in it because her mother is one of those mothers who never throws anything out. Because she loves Shawna. Whenever Shawna looks at Ellison she feels sorry for her because Shawna's mother is awesome and Ellison's mother is dead.

Shawna was observing how much bigger her teenage clothes were and she was feeling good that she is three or four sizes smaller now, depending on the store, and then she looked down and noticed a cardboard box. She opened it, and saw it was full of raw feelings in the form of ink that she had bent into words forever staining the pages of about twenty Hilroy notebooks. A younger and more innocent version of her had whimsically decorated them in a collage style with cut-out fashion-magazine pictures such as ladies' lips or high heels or various beauty products, or else stickers of unicorns in sad or noble poses that were both embarrassingly clichéd and emotionally triggering.

She started reading. At first she was entranced by how cute she used to be, with all of her naïve musings about life. But as she went along, there was a lot of stuff about how much she weighed and how much heavier she used to be. And she'd made all these lists of the foods she'd eaten, and rated each food on a scale of one to ten, one being the unhealthiest and ten being the healthiest. And at the end of a given day she would tally up those numbers and either celebrate her willpower or call herself a useless fat cow who deserved to drown in her own puke, or something similar.

When Adult Shawna read that, she touched the paper and traced those awful words that Teenage Shawna had written. She wished she could go back in time and hug her younger, chubbier self and reassure her that everything would be okay, and tell her that in the future she'd be way slimmer and would end up marrying a musician who often said she was beautiful.

A bunch of terrible things have happened to Ellison recently, which helps to put things in perspective. Shawna certainly doesn't feel happy that right before Ellison started making her newest record, her parents died, and then her cat died right after that. She of course takes less than zero delight in the unusual details of those events, in which the parents were buried alive in a freak mudslide in Bolivia and the cat got run over by an ice cream truck. Indeed, Shawna often thinks to herself, *Which of those deaths is more tragic?* Because obviously a cat can be replaced. But the thing was, Ellison had actually flagged down the ice cream truck herself because she was craving a cone. The guy came to a halt in front of her house, and guess who ran under the tires just at that moment? Yep. Not Ellison's parents. Shawna wonders, *Did she still order her frozen treat at that point?* Probably not. Those cones are never any good, anyway, from those trucks. Shawna used to like them, but not anymore.

It's a comforting realization for an ordinary, run-of-the-mill person like Shawna to think that super-rich and famous headliners are only human after all. Although ultimately Ellison rebounded and funnelled her pain into her music and became even more successful than before. She also wrote a memoir about the experience that became an instant bestseller. And while she was at it, she suddenly became an expert on nutrition. Ellison explained to all the talk-show hosts that she'd sworn off ice cream forever after her cat got run over, but still had a gigantic sweet tooth, so she hunkered down and wrote another book, a collection of "innocent-pleasure" recipes called *Healthy Indulgences*, that also flew off the shelves. Shawna bought that one because it sounded interesting, but she found the instructions way too complicated, and went back to having nonfat cottage cheese with cinnamon for dessert.

Shawna used to eat junk food all the time. It's so clear to her now that she was just trying to fill a huge emotional hole that could never possibly be filled, until she met Danny and he filled that hole with his love, which is unconditional, except for how he expects Shawna to give him at least one blow job per week. But she feels like that's a fair request, because he could be asking for five or ten.

He never makes comments about her weight. She appreciates this, even though technically there's nothing major to comment on now. She knows she could still lose a few pounds, but she's in the best shape she's ever been in thanks to all the exercising she does now. Shawna's newest thing is Pilates, although the Eastern European instructor is kind of mean because Shawna keeps asking her to correct her technique and she never does. She says Shawna should be able to just feel that the poses are correct with her own body. Shawna will say, "But I'm feeling this strain in my lower back," and the instructor will reply, "Then you're doing it wrong. And if you keep doing it wrong, you could get a severe spinal injury." There's all this crazy equipment and the other day Shawna sort of got twisted in a weird way, only slightly, but she still cried out in momentary pain, and she could've sworn the instructor smiled but then she covered her mouth with her hand.

Despite all the hard work, the other day when Shawna was at a corner store picking up cereal and condoms for the guys, she caught herself appraising the food products on the shelves, assigning numbers to everything like she used to do in her diaries. To make herself stop, she had to tell herself, out loud, "Stop." The lady behind the cash register frowned at her when she said it, and Shawna wanted to punch her in her scrawny, judgmental face, but she didn't.

And lately, whenever she sits down, her hands automatically go to the very slight roll of flesh that pops out over her waistband. Then she sort of palpates it, like a doctor would. But with a little bit of hate in her heart, which she assumes a doctor wouldn't have.

Still, Shawna figures that as long as she keeps moving and taking classes and maybe dropping another size or two, she'll be fine. And in any case she mostly likes how clothes fit her now, and occasionally Danny will say something like, "Damn, Shawna, you look good in those jeans," and she'll be happy for the rest of the day.

She appreciates him so much, because none of her past

boyfriends ever gave her compliments. She thinks maybe that was because she didn't used to be very attractive, but then why were they even with her in the first place, if they weren't attracted to her? It's also really validating that Danny actually married her, and continues to be satisfied in their marriage now that he's actually entered the music business, and as a result is constantly surrounded by temptation.

Last night Shawna was on the stage, over to the one side behind the curtain where the wives and girlfriends get to stand, and she was looking at all the women in the audience. Many of them were quite a bit older than she is but they were still women, and they were all watching Danny. And she started thinking that maybe she didn't look as good as she'd thought earlier in the evening when she got dressed for the show. Like maybe her shiny skirt was too tight, instead of being form-fitting as she would've originally described it.

At that point, she became preoccupied with thinking about how she should exercise more and eat less, and how she could change her diet so she could lose a bit more weight. Because more weight can always be lost. And while Shawna is skinnier now than she's ever been, she doesn't think anyone would actually use the word "skinny" to describe her.

Shawna is pretty sure that Ellison has never been anything other than skinny her entire long life. She is tiny, even. Shawna has always thought that tiny would be such a wonderful thing to be. To have people look at her and comment, "Oh, she's so tiny!"

She remembers when Danny first told her that his band was going to open for Ellison's band. He was drunk and horny and all over her and his hands were squeezing her butt, which she loves but she also hates because it reminds her that she has that much butt for him to squeeze. It feels like he wants to remind her, *Ooh, look at this big, yummy butt!* Which is sort of a compliment, but mostly not. It's not as if he's actually ever uttered those specific words, but sometimes he thinks them so hard that Shawna can feel them oozing out of his head. Those imaginary words can hurt.

So he was sort of kneading her butt like it was a giant lump of dough, and then he licked the sweat off her back, which admittedly was sexy but at the same time made her self-conscious about her sweating, which happens to her even with minor exertions. Although she used to be a lot sweatier in her heavier days, so that's another thing she's proud of, that she weighs less now so her body doesn't get overheated like it used to due to all the previous excess weight. But then Danny had to go and lick some sweat off her back and bang! she was right back there with those boyfriends from her past who used to say things to her such as, "Do you know there are some beaches in Greece where you wouldn't even be allowed to go, because they don't let fat people on those beaches?"

And then Danny was moaning, but then he stopped, and Shawna was like, "What? What happened? Did you go already?" She didn't think that was likely, since usually he can last forever, which is a blessing in one way but in another way it can actually be exhausting and annoying. Because mostly Shawna doesn't get to the finish line herself, and she's generally fine with that, but sometimes she'll be lying there getting pounded and feeling like, *Okay, I'm tired now.* And then finally he'll go, and afterwards he'll roll over and throw his arm around her middle, which is nice, because she's still so self-conscious of that area. No matter how much she exercises, that area still stays pretty soft. But when he puts his arm around her like that after sex, she hardly thinks of it at all, and she sometimes even sucks it in and looks down at herself and admires the contours of her sucked-in middle and thinks, *It's so much smaller than it's ever been.*

But in this case, he was moaning way too early, so Shawna asked him, "Danny, are you okay?"

And he said, "Yeah. I just re-remembered something that made me so happy."

And she said, "What is it?" Thinking maybe he was remembering the first time he met her, or something.

He said, "I wanted to give you a massive orgasm first, so you could feel the same basic sensations I'm feeling right now in this very instant."

She said, "That's nice. But why don't you just go ahead and tell me?"

Instead of describing the moment he'd first laid eyes on Shawna, he related the story about meeting Ellison earlier that day. The details were familiar, because as it turned out, he'd first laid eyes on Ellison in the exact same place, doing the exact same thing, where he'd first met Shawna all those years ago: busking outside the bank where she works.

He said he and the guys were killing it, just nailing it so hard they even had a medium-sized crowd around them, and then this tiny lady with giant hair walked by with this entourage of, like, twenty guys, and the lady stopped walking and held up a tiny hand with these perfectly painted, pointy red nails and said, "Everybody, hang on! I want to hear this."

So the whole gang of them stopped and they all stood around and listened to Danny and the guys finishing up "You Say Go But I Say Don't Go, So Where Does That Leave Us? Right Here I Guess." Danny said at first he didn't know who she was, even though he definitely recognized her as someone famous and musical and kept thinking, *Who is she?* And then it came to him, and he was so shocked that he almost broke a guitar string, but he didn't, which was a relief because strings are expensive.

When they were done their set, this tiny woman with huge hair clapped her tiny manicured hands, and her gang of large men clapped their big hands too, and then she said, "My name is Ellison and I'm going on tour with my new album and I want you guys to be my opener."

They were all like, *Holy shit, this is Ellison? Ellison just listened to us and then clapped for us?* Because she looked so much bigger on her album covers, and here she was so tiny, like a doll, a Barbie doll even, because of her curvy proportions but overall smallness and smoothness.

Danny had nodded and closed his eyes when he related that part to Shawna. In response, her hand snaked all over her own naked body and she made a mental note of all the places where it was not smooth, but was in fact lumpy. But she didn't say that out loud, and even if she had, Danny probably would've told her to shut up, she was being silly, she was gorgeous, and he knew it and she knew it. So just thinking that he would probably say that made her feel better.

Still, Shawna was not feeling too good about all the times Danny had used the word "tiny" in his descriptions of Ellison. It sort of put her in an overall bad mood. Of course, she was trying hard to be happy for this wonderful news that her husband was so excitedly relaying, concerning the future of his hardworking but as-yet-unappreciated band getting potentially brighter. This had implications for the brightness of their own shared future as well, meaning maybe a big enough combined income that would allow them to discuss having a child. Shawna isn't sure she wants a child, but it's nice to consider another chapter of their life together potentially unfolding like a napkin on her lap when she and Danny go to a restaurant to celebrate their love.

And then Shawna said, "Wait a minute, you met her outside my bank but you didn't come in after and tell me?"

And Danny said, "I totally would've, babe, but she invited me and the guys out for lunch and we all went to that pub around the corner that you like and we shared some wings and drank a few pints and then I just came home and met up with you here."

So now they're on tour with Ellison, which is insane. To go from busking outside a bank to playing sold-out stadium shows with a premium, seasoned singer with millions of fans. Even if those fans are different from the fans who'd be going to see, say, a younger band. Meaning the people who attend Ellison's concerts are all of a certain age, which is fine, because older people are the only ones who have enough money to afford her ticket prices. But eventually her fans are going to die, and then where will she be? Also dead, probably. Not really a problem for Ellison in that case.

But when Shawna looks at the situation from The Cheat-o's point of view, attaching themselves to a musician who is just going to die in, like, ten or fifteen years isn't the best career move. So lately she's been saying to Danny that they should think about branching out, to be seen as more than just an opener. But he and the guys seem pretty content with the situation they've got going. One of the perks is, there's a lot of booze, which was something they already enjoyed in their pre-Ellison days, but now it's free so they enjoy it even more.

The other night, everybody was out drinking, Danny's band and Ellison's band and all the girlfriends and wives, but no boyfriend or husband because Ellison is single, which is sad, especially for a forty-something-year-old lady. She looks a lot younger, so Shawna always wonders why she doesn't have a special guy in her life. Or a special woman, although everybody says Ellison likes men, especially younger men who are already in relationships.

They were at the bar and Ellison came up to Shawna and said, "Shawna, I had this totally crazy dream last night. I was having dinner with Danny after a show, just the two of us, but of course it was totally innocent, obviously. And then you suddenly barged into the restaurant all enraged, like you'd caught us doing something wrong. And the next thing I knew, you wrapped your hands around my neck and your nails were razor-sharp and you started squeezing and I couldn't breathe and your razor-sharp nails pierced my skin and blood started spurting out. I looked into your eyes, which were black as the Devil, and I gurgled, 'Why, Shawna, why?' And you said, 'Because I hate you, Ellison.' It was a really intense dream, whew." Then she just walked away. Shawna stood there, staring after her. And all she could think was, *But I always thought the Devil was red.*

Then she started feeling bad about all the beer she'd consumed, and the shots of butterscotch schnapps as well, which were delicious but had to contain, like, ten grams of sugar each, at least. Her hands went to that little flesh roll on top of her waistband, and stayed there.

So now Shawna is kind of cursing herself for reading those teenage diaries because clearly they brought a bunch of old bad habits back, and old bad feelings too. Food has started calling to her more insistently, like it used to. She had finally reached the point where she could ignore that call, and eventually she didn't even hear it at all, except when her stomach was actually rumbling due to real, biological hunger. But now donuts are singing to her from donut shops in their greasy little tempting donut voices, trying to lure her in. So far she's been able to resist, but for how much longer?

All those negative thoughts have been coming back at her like a crashing wave. Or, if you're Ellison's parents, a giant wall of mud. Is it cruel of Shawna to think of this? There's just something about Ellison that Shawna doesn't like.

Shawna of course appreciates that Ellison lets her stand off to the side of the stage for the concerts, even though the annoying sound guy always whisper-shouts at Shawna to step back a few paces because she's too obviously on the stage. And she shoots him this glare like, *Perhaps you don't remember, Andrew, but I'm Danny's fucking wife, who Danny married almost an entire year ago by saying the words "I do," and those words were in reference to me. And I was wearing a strapless gown and I looked beautiful and I wasn't even self-conscious about my armpit fat or anything.*

She knows he does remember. Andrew is at every show because he's been Ellison's sound guy forever, and his need to tell Shawna she should be more in the background pisses her off. Because she's always dressed nicely, and if she was this perfectly skinny stick figure then maybe he wouldn't make those comments to her, like maybe the audience would think she was a groupie who'd jumped up on stage, which could be dramatic and cool, instead of this regular-sized wife in a too-tight shiny skirt from Marshalls. Where's the exciting drama in that scenario, right?

Shawna is sick of the various men in her life telling her what to do and how to look. Like her last boyfriend, who — when they were out on a date, in public, in front of the waiter — would say things to her such as, "That's all you're going to eat? A big gal like you?" So Andrew can fuck right off and go back to his level-fixing or whatever the hell he does in his dumb job that anybody with a diploma from the DeVry Institute of Technology could do.

Danny, on the other hand, is a professional. He's good at what he does because he practises a lot. He's always been a very hopeful guy who thinks about life in a positive light. His dream has come true and he's living that dream, and as a bonus, Shawna gets to live it right along with him. Like this morning, for example, when they were cuddling in the king-sized bed in their fancy hotel room, and she'd told him about the video she'd shot of the show, and he'd wanted to see it.

After he'd watched the clip and said those nice things about it, he asked her, "How much vacation time do you have left, again?"

And she said, "I have to go back next week, remember?"

And he said, "Oh yeah, I forgot."

And Shawna said, "Are you going to miss me?"

And Danny said, "Of course I will."

Then he told her that he and Ellison had made some plans to go out for dinner that night, and said he'd totally invite her along but it was going to be really boring because it was a business meeting and they were only going to talk about work stuff, and work stuff was boring, right?

To which Shawna replied, "Yeah, I'd rather just stay in the hotel room and watch *The Bachelor* anyway."

He smiled at her. "Taking a little Shawna-time, huh?"

She smiled back at him. "Exactly."

And he said, "Cool."

And she said, "Cool." She pulled the covers up over herself and said, "I'm hungry."

And Danny said, "Let's order room service because room

service is sexy. And so are you. And don't worry, I'll tell them to cook your egg-white omelette without butter and leave the cream out of your oatmeal. I know how you like it, baby."

And then he kissed her.

And okay, it wasn't exactly the type of kiss she'd been waiting for her whole life. But it was pretty damn close.

# REAL LIFE

SHE SEES HIM THROUGH the window when he steps outside to have a smoke. It's that actor who played a sexy role on a TV show she used to watch sometimes late at night when her husband was asleep. His character was in a conflicted relationship with the female star's character. They were on-again-off-again, yet they understood each other on a deeply intimate level.

The actor has pointy ears and a morose expression, like an emotionally wounded elf. His features overall are quite delicate, though still extremely masculine. He sucks on his cigarette and blows out a big white cloud that makes the whole scene very storybook-like. Then he comes back inside and sits at the bar. Now she is fully aware that he is here, drinking a beer in the same establishment she is drinking a beer in.

She wonders if he likes the music they're playing, because she is really enjoying it. She has grooved to every single song so far. They have all been from the era when she was in university and danced a lot and felt free and unencumbered. Her heart was so light back then that she would occasionally braid her short hair and secure the braids with tiny multi-coloured elastics.

She thinks about approaching the actor and making an insightful comment about the amazing tunes. It would have to be insightful because strangers probably say stupid things to him constantly, and he needs to know she's different. She could offer him a profound observation such as, "Grunge really gets you all revved up and ready to drink and party." And he would agree. Because who doesn't like grunge? Murderers, maybe.

He's watching the TV mounted over the bar, which is playing a strange cartoon that looks familiar to her. A dolphin and a hedgehog live together in a cramped apartment and they don't get along very well. The hedgehog is uppity and the dolphin is filled with bitterness. The sound is muted, so she can't hear what the dolphin is shouting as he shoves the hedgehog up against a wall and rams his dorsal fin into his roommate's soft, exposed belly.

The actor is still wearing his retro-type ski jacket even though he's inside. It's red and black and too tight on him, like he's outgrown it. It only partially covers his bum. She has not seen his bare bum on TV — it isn't that kind of show. It isn't a family show, but it isn't racy enough to have a bare bum in it. Once, though, he wore a dog collar in a dream sequence where the lead actress was having a hot fantasy about him.

He heads to the men's room and leaves his beer sitting on the bar. She wonders if he ever worries about that, if somebody will put drugs in his drink to make him sleep with them and do things with them, against his will but not really because hey, he's a guy, and guys are always up for sex. They'll do it with any-body, it doesn't matter, even a person like her who is married so she's the one who would be breaking vows, not him. The only negative aspect in that type of sex deal would be that he might be concerned about diseases after, but then she could tell him she was married so he would be reassured.

The problem is, she keeps having this dream where she falls out of love with her husband. He doesn't do anything wrong, he just stops being attractive to her. She tries and tries to get the love back, but it's gone. And then there's another guy, she meets him in the dream during some sort of adventure she's on with her husband. The adventure varies. Sometimes it's a safari, sometimes they're bank robbers, sometimes they're escaping a dinosaur attack. She and her husband are all caught up in the action, and the other guy has a job that fits him into the plot somehow, like he's a lion specialist or the chief of police or a dinosaur specialist.

The actor comes back from the men's room and sits down at the bar again. He finishes his beer and orders another one. He likes beer, that's for sure.

She could say to him, "Aren't beer and music great?" And then, "It's okay, I'm clean — the only other guy I sleep with is my husband, but we hardly ever do it anymore because doing it causes us to recall that at one point we tried to have kids but it didn't work out. We had wished to experience together the joy of being parents, but when it all flopped we had to make our peace with that reality. Because apparently his sperm is not very effective at getting me pregnant. So don't worry about it."

In the dream, her husband realizes she doesn't love him anymore and he cries. His crying is the worst. Early on in their relationship (in real life, not the dream) they had a miscommunication about a surprise party he was organizing for his mother's birthday. He hadn't actually asked her to attend, and yet he kept blabbing on about this dumb party and all the dumb party plans he was making. She thought if he didn't want her there then fine, but just stop talking about it all the time! One day he showed her a website for a company that manufactured personalized piñatas shaped like the to-be-celebrated person's greatest fear, so that the act of smashing it would be extra cathartic. He said, "I think it's rodeo clowns but it might also be getting her face chewed by rats. Maybe they could combine those somehow?" And she said, "We have to talk." He slumped, and his eyes morphed into empty pools reflecting papier mâché mushroom clouds, parakeets, the Ebola virus. She understood then with unshakeable certainty that his greatest fear was a life without her, and that she was invited.

Up on the TV, the dolphin and the hedgehog are fighting again. She remembers now why it's so familiar — a few times she fell asleep watching the actor's show, and when she was startled awake in the middle of the night, this cartoon was playing. The experience was disorienting and reminded her of sleepwalking as a child. Once, she woke up in front of the television in her parents' rec room. She was wearing her favourite blue nightie with the dancing bears, and onscreen a tall man with a black beard was strapping a screaming woman onto a table that had spikes on it.

The premise of the cartoon seems to be that the dolphin and the hedgehog were friends when they moved in together but then ended up hating each other. All because of a few simple but hilarious misunderstandings, and due to the fact that the dolphin is cranky all the time because he's slowly dying from being on land. "This apartment is so dry!" he shouts, and the laugh track goes crazy.

She saw another famous person once, walking on the side-walk, as she and her husband were passing the bulk food store. She said to her husband, "If you still want the onion powder, we could get it now," and right at that moment, she saw the hand-some carpenter from the hardware store commercials who shows novice homeowners how to fix all the terrible things that can go wrong with their properties using tools that are on sale that week. And she physically swooned. There he was, with his massive square shoulders and hands like pie plates, strolling along the same pavement she was strolling along, and suddenly she was breathing faster and felt lightheaded. She thought, *I am swooning.* Then her husband said, "No, it's okay. We're probably fine for a little while longer."

She could say to the actor now, "This is just a special thing between us that nobody else has to know about. I'm a big fan of that sexy character you play on TV but I am fully aware you're a separate person from that in real life, with your own unique aversions and desires. I don't expect you to be able to spin around and suddenly you're in another dimension because that's the magical ability you have on the show. I know that stuff's all fake. I'm not an insane person! Really, though, you should be flattered that ordinary people like me know who you are and recognize you when you're out in public. And you shouldn't look so forlorn like a stag being pursued by hunters all the time. That stuff is for the jerks of high school, but you are a grown man with a coveted job in the entertainment industry. If you had any sense, you would show some gratitude so your fans can see you're content with your life that is charmed in a way that theirs will never be."

Her husband is nice but he has a way of ruining things for her. One time she wanted to share a muffin with him as a romantic gesture. It was a sunny day and they were in Loblaws, and there were all these muffins. She selected a blueberry-flax one that was moist and indulgent with bonus health benefits, but when her husband took a bite he frowned and said, "All I can taste is the baking soda."

Most regular non-actors are subject to endless daily disappointments, so when every once in a while they get to glimpse someone who is more golden than them, having all of these advantages like superior chiselled jawbones and being on a TV show, they go away from the encounter with the hopeful feeling that maybe they should treat themselves to a triple-ounce mango Bellini. So what the fuck is wrong with this actor, to not understand this dynamic?

One time the dream about her husband was subtly different, in that she actually had sex with the other guy in it. The act itself was nothing over the top — just two people having basic intercourse. She did notice, though, that the guy's body was long and sleek and had flippers. Afterwards she had a lot of regret.

But her memory of the event was foggy, as if she'd been under a spell. Then she realized a spell was exactly what had occurred — this other guy was a mythical half-seal-half-man creature, and he had bewitched her! She gave her husband this explanation. He said, "You mean a selkie?" He didn't seem too upset, but that was when she woke up, so maybe she missed the part where he became furious and asked for a divorce.

The waitress is putting candles on the tables now because it's getting dark out. Normally this is just one of those bars with chicken fingers and sweet potato fries on the menu and some sports décor and posters of Ireland, but the flickering flames give the room an air of enchantment. It would be the perfect time to go over and tell the actor that she recognizes him from that show: "And you're one of my favourite characters! Like that time when the plot involved you finally sleeping with the female star, I was excited to see you take off your shirt. Your chest was skinny and not as impressive as I'd anticipated, but your arms were ultra-ideal examples of primitive sinew and muscle."

One time she did a pregnancy test in the ladies' room of this bar. She sat on the toilet in the left-hand stall and ripped open the packet with her teeth. She peed on the plastic stick which was a beautiful light violet, the sort of colour she'd paint her daughter's room if she had a daughter. Purple was feminine but not in-your-face feminine like pink, which had gotten out of control these days. They were making pink Lego for girls! What was wrong with multi-coloured Lego? If she had a daughter, she would tell her that blue wasn't only for boys, and vice versa about pink if she had a son. She would teach him or her to appreciate the genderless beauty of a summer breeze on their small, flaw-less face.

The music stops all of a sudden and a few people go, "Hey, hey!" But the bartender shouts, "Wait, wait! I love this bit!" He jerks up the volume on the TV right as the hedgehog starts screaming at the dolphin, "You don't get me! You have never gotten me! I always have to explain myself to you!"

She wonders if children watch this cartoon. If she watched it when she was a little girl, it would have made her cry.

The problem is, babies get older and they learn things. They go to sleepovers and watch grown-up movies and TV and become wise about the adult parts of life. So it's probably just as well that she doesn't have some junior know-it-all around. Plus her husband has easily clogged Eustachian tubes, which would not be a good trait to pass down to a child. Even the smallest amount of wax will irritate them and cause them to become inflamed. Sometimes they are swollen for days.

Of all people, this actor should really feel a lot more thrilled to be alive. Certainly all human beings are miracles but he in particular is an extra-special miracle with his successful acting career and youthful good looks. Because while he may be all world-weary on the show, in reality he's just a kid.

She thinks, *I am older and wiser than you, and I could make you feel better. I would try my best to cheer you up.* She would tell the actor that life is meant to be savoured, even if all you ever do is go to a boring job and say hi and bye to people you don't like much, but they're in charge of your paycheque and they delegate tasks to you which you have to complete in order to pay your bills. She would buy him a drink or maybe see if he wanted to buy her a drink instead, she being the woman in the equation.

After she did that pregnancy test — which was the last of many pregnancy tests over the years, because those things are expensive if they're not on sale — she gave up on the whole motherhood thing. She decided to embrace the life she had and the freedom that childlessness affords the childless, and she walked out of the ladies' room into the bar and ordered a bunch of shots. Later on, when she was close to passing out but not yet ready to vomit, an old man with a beard put his long arm around her shoulders and asked what she was celebrating. She kissed his cheek and shouted, "Just the greatness of it all!" And she let out a whoop and the old man and several other patrons whooped too and raised their glasses high in the air. Nobody was left out and they all came together like a family.

The actor orders another beer for himself and leaves it sitting there again while he heads outside to have another smoke. If he were just a little older, he might already know some of the valuable truths she has learned about the world, in this bar and beyond. But he isn't so he doesn't, and that's all right. She loves him anyway.

## GAZEBO TIMES

A MAN STARTS WAVING a gun around when Conrad is on his break.

Conrad only gets a half-hour for lunch, which is stupid. That's barely enough time to grab a burger from the burger place and take the escalator up to the next floor and find a free spot on a bench and sit down to enjoy his meal. And then it takes him one or two minutes to get his headphones out of his bag and put them on, but obviously that has to happen because being on break means he gets to listen to music instead of listening to all the stupid idiots in the mall like he has to do for the rest of the time.

Conrad works at the falafel stand. All day long he drops chickpea balls into boiling oil and then he squashes each one with a fork before adding the toppings and sauces. He only squashes them a little bit, though, because if he squashes them too much, the customers will complain that the ball doesn't look like a ball anymore, it looks more like a squashed thing that they don't want to eat.

He used to squash the falafel balls way too much, but then he learned.

The purpose of the squashing is so the tahini can penetrate the crunchy fried outer shell of the falafel. It's a special technique invented by the owner. And yet the customers don't know that Conrad and the rest of the staff are trying their best to give them the tastiest lunch possible. They have no idea.

While Conrad is upstairs eating his burger, which he prefers to falafels because it's meat, the workers at the choose-your-own salad place take shelter under their gleaming white counter. The workers at the burger place can't hide because somebody's trademark paper hat with the cartoon of the dancing all-beef patty has fallen onto the grill and started to smoke. That cartoon always makes Conrad smile when he sees it. It's this sort of oblong brown lump with little legs and arms twirling around under a disco ball, which is funny. And Conrad knows comedy.

Right now, though, Conrad isn't smiling. On top of having to rush to eat his food, he has to rush even more today because he has to go and buy baby wipes. His pregnant wife told him to. So now he has to figure out what store would sell baby wipes. A store that sells clothes for babies? Who knows? Plus why does she need baby wipes when they don't even have a baby yet?

Back in the food court, the man holding the gun steps up onto a formed plastic table in the middle of all the other formed plastic tables and says, "Today is a good day to walk your dog if you have a dog. If you don't have a dog, then God help you. I got my first dog when I was three. That's young to have a dog. But my mother and father thought that having a pet would teach me a thing or two about the world. One day I decided to see how long my dog, which was a little dog because I was a little boy, could hold his breath underwater. We made a game of it. I said, 'It's time for your bath, Moonbeam!' Moonbeam was the name of my little dog. I thought of it because I had always liked moonbeams. I said, 'Look, it's nice in the water!' I made as if to get in the bathtub myself. I was just faking, though."

Early that morning there had been a meeting of all the food-court workers, and Conrad had walked away from the meeting feeling really good because they'd learned that a gazebo would soon be installed in the collective outdoor break area. There were already four picnic tables out there, in the rectangle of grass between the delivery zone and the garbage bins. On pleasant-weather days it was a pretty big deal to score a seat on one of those picnic tables.

But now there would be another spot for the workers to sit and rest and eat their lunches and talk about what they liked and didn't like about their families, and in this case there would also be shade from the sun when it was sunny. There was already some shade under an overhanging metal sheet that nobody knew the reason for — it just hung there providing shade — but hey, nobody was complaining.

Right now, although it was winter, Conrad was looking forward to sitting in the gazebo in the spring and talking about his baby, who was going to be born soon and then Conrad would be a father, which was absolutely crazy when he really took the time to think about it.

Over by the falafel stand, Conrad's wife goes into labour.

Her water breaks and floods around her shoes. She had arrived secretly at the mall to surprise him and thought it would be nice to shop for baby wipes together, but unfortunately she arrived too late.

The food-court workers had been given an artist's rendering of the gazebo to pass around — "to get you guys super psyched," said the mall manager, who had a time-share in Mexico that she liked to tell everybody about. Then she'd always say, "There are way more tourists than Mexicans so crime isn't a problem. The only problem is what to do with all that tequila! Ha ha ha." The circular roofed structure in the drawing was breathtaking, with stately latticework and whimsical curlicues and a jaunty spike at the top.

The gazebo had a maximum capacity so there would only be space for six food-court workers to enjoy it at once. There would be a sign-up sheet by the lockers where employees could put their names. The sign-up sheet would be refreshed daily and would have the title "Gazebo Times."

Conrad's wife shrieks, and the man with the gun tells her to be quiet because he has a headache.

Conrad became temporarily famous the previous year. He co-wrote a live comedy sketch about doing an intervention on a baby who is drinking too much breast milk. At the time he didn't plan on becoming a parent but he had friends who were parents, and they had gotten kind of boring, but their infants gave him all sorts of amusing ideas.

The way the sketch went was there's a guy playing the baby by sucking his thumb and saying, "Goo goo, ga ga!" over and over.

Then a bunch of people crowd into the room, including the man who is playing the mother by wearing a bra hilariously stuffed with balloons. Somebody says to the baby, "Okay Joe, you'd better sit down for this." Which is part of the humour because babies are always sitting down! Or else lying down. The interveners all stand around what is supposed to be the crib but is actually just a pile of chairs arranged to be crib-like. The best thing about live comedy is you create a reality out of thin air. There are hardly any props, only the sheer talent of the actors involved to help the audience see the world they have brought to life.

The man with the gun says he's hungry and will somebody please bring him some fries. Nobody volunteers, so he points his gun at Conrad's wife and shouts, "Now will somebody bring me some goddamn fries?" A frantic whispering spreads through the food court, becoming louder and more insistent. Eventually the guy who sold Conrad his burger scurries over with a trademark paper cone full of golden fries, and he pees his pants when he hands it to the man with the gun.

The man frowns at the cartoon of the dancing potato on the cone and says, "Is this supposed to be funny? Because it's not." Then Conrad's wife loses her balance and falls into the puddle at her feet, and the man says, "Now that's funny." He sticks a few fries into his mouth and chews. "My parents loved me a lot," he says. "And I have always enjoyed those perfect-weather days when the sun is shining and the dog parks are full of dogs. You say you are a cat person? Get out of my face. I don't want to talk to you. Just the other day I saw a cat and I kicked it straight in the head. That was for trying to come inside my house. This cat had tried that trick on me before. It succeeded once, and I said, 'If you don't get out, you'll find out pretty quick there's a dog in here.' I have a big dog now, he is a big, curly dog. I pretend his curls are rings and I stick my hands deep into his coat and then I have rings on all my fingers, like Liberace." The man eats a few more fries and says, "You should know another thing about me: I am not into jewellery, because jewellery is for women. But just with my dog's fur I like to pretend."

On the floor in front of the falafel stand, Conrad's wife lies on her side in a pool of amniotic fluid that grows larger until it surrounds her like a miniature lake. Her clothes are soaked and even her hair is wet now and she wants to reach up and wring it out, but the man with the gun is watching her so she doesn't do anything.

In the comedy sketch, the guy playing the baby sort of blinks around at the people who are supposed to be his concerned father and older siblings and grandparents. The interveners put on serious faces and take turns telling the baby that they are very worried about his health and well-being because of his excessive breast-milk drinking.

Conrad's wife is one of those lucky pregnant women who does not look like she's going to give birth imminently. She's always been small, and throughout her pregnancy she would get nasty looks from other women who were secretly jealous of her smallness but to her face they would say, "Are you sure your baby's getting enough food in there?" The contractions are more painful now but she tries not to move or make any sounds. She wonders if she's having a boy or a girl. She only has a girl's name picked out so far because she is really hoping for a daughter. But of course as long as the child is healthy, that's the most important thing. And she is going to be a way better mother than her cousin Patricia, who lets her eight-year-old daughter go to sleepovers at her friends' houses even when Patricia doesn't know the parents very well. And one time Conrad's wife said, "Patricia, how can you let her spend the night with these adults who are basically strangers? Don't you think that's unsafe?" And Patricia said, "Oh, they're fine. It's nice to have the house to ourselves once in a while. You'll understand when you're a mom." But Conrad's wife doesn't think she will.

The sketch was such a hit that audiences started yelling out requests for it during shows that had totally different themes, and the actors started tossing dollar-store bibs out into the crowd at the end of the night. It became a phenomenon — audience members would stream out of the comedy club wearing these cheap bibs, which were too tight on their fully grown necks. The bib-wearers on Twitter would tweet about it immediately — I got a bib! #comedybib — and the ones not on Twitter would tell their friends about it later — "I got a bib!" "What kind of bib?" "A comedy bib!" "Fucking right on." Eventually people got tired of it, though, because people always get tired of things.

Conrad finishes his burger and feels disappointed that it wasn't as good as usual. The normally charred bits weren't charred enough this time. He crumples the wrapper and wipes his mouth with it because he forgot to get a napkin. Then he sits and tries to remember what else he was supposed to do on his break. Because there was definitely something.

# WE WISH YOU HAPPINESS,
## WITH ALL YOUR FRIENDS AROUND

FIRST, A BAD FEELING, but it goes away. Because hey, they're at the beach.

She hands him her sketchbook, reclines on the rented plastic lounger. "Draw me."

He flicks the pen against her bare leg. "You know I'm no good at this."

THEY WEREN'T A COUPLE anymore but they'd already booked their flight, so they went to Italy anyway.

When they arrived, the heat was unbearable, but they figured at least they'd have their own private language for covert emotional jabs. Unfortunatcly, it seemed that almost everyone spoke some English, which meant they couldn't say mean things to each other without strangers knowing. So in public, they were perfect.

"You go first," he'd say to her.

"No, you," she'd say to him.

And they'd stand there until someone else opened the door.

HE SQUINTS AT HER, at the page. "I can't get your nose right."

She sighs, tries to peek. "You're always rushing things."

"Close your eyes, it's easier for me that way. I don't have to see the malice in them. Malice is hard to reproduce."

She lowers her lids and plucks at her swimsuit, snaps it against her skin. "You have to focus on the lines, I told you."

Scattered Italian phrases. She concentrates, waiting for something recognizable — a *prego* or a *grazie*.

Some things were easier to understand when she wasn't looking.

On the plane, for instance, she knew even in her sleep when it was mealtime.

She was dreaming that she was wearing a beautiful dress made out of real red roses, and she twirled around in it for him.

He frowned, which wasn't the reaction she wanted. "A dress made from flowers isn't very practical. You'll need to watch out for bees."

"But it smells so nice," she said.

"No, it doesn't." He plugged his nose. "Take a whiff."

And right then the ruthless, tangy arrival of chicken cacciatore burned the dream away and blasted them both apart as the scrinching of cellophane came down the aisle like a wave.

"Wow, look how choppy the water is," he says now. "No, never mind, keep your eyes shut. I've almost got it."

She opens them for a moment, just to annoy him, before she complies.

On the other side of them, a little boy in a purple Speedo digs a hole while his sunburnt parents toast each other with sparkling cans of Peroni.

EVERY NIGHT, HER ARMS fell asleep. She'd wake up with them numb and tingling over her head. She had to lay them at her sides until the blood flowed back and the tingling stopped.

Every morning, the alarm. They were unsure if it was okay to sleep in, because it didn't feel okay. It didn't feel okay to sleep together either, but there was only one bed in the apartment they'd rented, and neither of them wanted to sleep on the couch.

There was a nursery school behind them, so the longer they stayed inside, the longer they had to listen to the shrieks of laughter and howls of outrage from children they couldn't even see.

"Jesus," he'd said the first time they heard it. "Let's get out of here."

They'd left in search of macchiato, their shared need for caffeine briefly uniting them. On their way they'd walk past the school gates, where dozens of naked toddler bums winked at them through the bars. Sliding down slides, swinging on swings, playing in the sandbox.

"What the hell?" He shook his head. "Why would they put them on display like that for perverts to gawk at?"

She said, "They're much freer with their bodies here. You have to leave the North American mindset behind." She was proud that she was already fitting in much better than he was. "Didn't your parents let you run around without clothes on when you were little?"

He shrugged. "I can't remember that far back."

HE PUTS HIS DRAWING of her face down on his towel when it's time for lunch. They're having a picnic. It's the end of their trip and they are finally relaxing.

To celebrate, they spent too much on a rental car to get to the beach. Now they're eating oily cheese cubes and pouring warm wine into plastic cups that already have sand in them. She asks him if he's enjoying himself, and he says why wouldn't he be.

Across the beach, whoops and hollers. A whole bunch of people are having a really good time.

He says, "Must be a volleyball net over there."

She says, "What makes you think they're playing sports? Maybe they're excited about something else."

He says, "Nobody gets that excited about anything other than sports."

She tears a puff of bread out of the loaf they'd packed. They hadn't sliced it in advance because they thought it would be more fun to rip pieces off, but now all that's left is a caved-in crust. And even when she chews carefully, the grit in her teeth makes a horrible scraping noise she wants to run and hide from.

THEY WERE IN A foreign land and the apartment had a weak Internet connection. They started to feel carefree, far away from the crush of sympathetic head-shakes and shoulder pats, all the solidarity "likes" on Facebook.

He didn't always wash his fruit before biting into it, and she didn't always apply sunblock more than once a day.

Their windows had no screens, and they left them open and didn't even worry about birds flying in.

Until one did, and they found it with a broken neck on the floor.

He said, "Should this go in with the organics?"

She said, "You figure it out."


HIS PEN MOVES ACROSS the paper again, and he asks her, "What would make you happy, right now?"

Shouting.

She shields her eyes against the raging sun with a flattened hand.

Running. A blur of tanned legs kicking up sand. More yelling down the beach, maybe twenty feet away. A commotion.

He puts down the pen. "I think something's happening over there."

She wants his arms around her. She says, "Right now, what would make me happy is a big, juicy peach. Did we pack any?"


THEY DID WHAT PEOPLE are supposed to do when they go to Rome. They filled their days with tours of the Forum, the Pantheon, the Colosseum, the Vatican. They threw coins into the Trevi Fountain. Small denominations only, because they weren't wishing for anything big.

He said, "Wow, there are so many historic buildings here."

She said, "You think?"

Then he stole a cloth napkin right off a table from an outdoor café and used it to mop up his sweat, and she said, "Can you get me one of those?" So he did.

They explored the local art galleries and found one that offered free olives in a bowl by the door. Was that sanitary? Who cared? They were on vacation.

They each took a handful and wandered around the white room admiring photos of baby pigs and real actual human babies, arranged side by side as if to highlight their similarities.

Later on, they ate way too much pasta.

BEACH UMBRELLAS LIKE SWIRLED gelato: grapefruit pink and lemon yellow, pistachio green and blood orange. A wall of bronzed backs, bathing suits in black, blue, silver.

She says, "It's like a painting."

Then a subtle rearranging, and more colours appear.

Purple Speedo. White T-shirt with red lettering. One set of small pink arms and legs fanned out and another set of larger limbs huddled over. Hands pressing down.

Women smoke cigarettes and cradle their infants. Men smoke cigarillos and bend their dark heads close to each other, humming concern.

Then there is a helicopter. It hovers and lands, drowning out all other sound. Even the waves, which were deafening before.

The wind from the rotors kicks up a cloud of sand, and they

both press their sunglasses more tightly against their faces to protect their eyes.

THE MORNING BEFORE, THE nursery-school children had put on a play for their parents.

The two of them spooned Nutella out of the jar and watched from their window even though they couldn't understand the words.

They figured out pretty easily, though, that the plot centred on an evil witch. Every time she cast one of her spells, she banged a drum in a threatening manner. Then she shouted, "Diddle-dee-yeehoo!" and the kids squealed like they were on fire.

After that, they spent the whole day inside, taking naps and drinking wine. They were so tired of the heat.

That night, the tiniest breeze blew into the apartment, and they sat at their wide-open window with their last bottle of plonk so they could feel all of it.

In one of the nearby apartments, a group of women was chanting, "Way weesh yoo heppy niss? Wittall. Yoor frenz. Ay-rown?"

There was something familiar about the sing-songy words. They had to close their eyes and listen for a long time before they figured it out.

He leaned closer to her, whispered, "They're practising."

She nodded, but leaned away from his breath, which was thick with the salty prosciutto they'd eaten earlier. That had been the only thing in their fridge besides two sad, wrinkled tomatoes, which should have been left to ripen on the counter instead.

Amidst the clinking of glasses and a few self-conscious giggles, the women repeated the sentence until it was only a collection of noises again.

THE TWO OF THEM stick to their plastic chairs beneath the sun, gummy with sweat. They are so hot and the ocean is so cool, but nobody is swimming now.

The crowd shuffles towards a kneeling man and woman. Heads shake, hands reach out to touch sunburnt shoulders. Then they close in, a barricade again. More Italian architecture for the tourists to puzzle over.

She's eating the peach, and feels guilty for enjoying it. She doesn't stop, though. She gobbles it up and buries the pit in the sand where nobody will see.

He returns to the notebook, frowning as he smudges the lines with his thumb.

A few minutes later, the helicopter lifts off and flies away, and everyone goes back to what they were doing before.

He says, "Whoa, that was pretty dramatic."

She starts to pack up.

Then he shows her the drawing, which is finished now. "What do you think?"

She leans in, examines his smiling version of her.

"Huh," she says, "it's actually pretty good."

# DUMPLING NIGHT

WE HAD THE WHOLE room. It was all ours, for the entire evening, and it was incredible. The wallpaper was gold. Not actual gold, but a very shiny facsimile. There was a pond in the middle. A pond! We were even told there had once been real fish inside.

If you have ever booked the Special Banquet Chamber at the Golden Dragon Palace out on Staynard and Highway 12, you will know what I'm talking about when I say that this semi-enclosed dining area was a mind-blower.

The best part: when we first arrived, Uncle Troy took me aside and delivered these instructions: "Glenn-o, somebody you don't know sticks his head in here, you look him in the eye and explain that this is a private party."

I pretend-saluted him, which was our thing, and said, "You can count on me, Uncle Troy."

I'm a pretty big guy, so I often find myself appointed as the unofficial doorman on these sorts of occasions. And if there's one thing I'm good at, it's telling people where they do and do not belong. I make my living by categorizing classified ads, and you would be amazed at the far-out notions certain individuals have about what sections their precious third-hand sofa-bed or expired coupon collection should be placed in.

It was Dumpling Night, and I know that because when I walked past the steam table, a teenage girl was there with tongs and she said, "Dumpling?"

I said, "What kind?"

She pointed to her apron, which was emblazoned with a cartoon creature resembling a giant, happy slug. "It's Dumpling Night." This didn't really answer my question, but at least I knew the score.

So I said, "Sure," and she plucked a shiny, puffy dough-ball from the steam table and deposited it on my plate.

I thanked her and proceeded to the salad bar for some salad items. I had already planned out what I was going to get: pickled beets, green olives, baby corn, water chestnuts, and sunflower seeds, although I was still working on the layering order. An important part of the equation was the tendency of beet juice to stain everything in its path.

I like buffets partly because of all the choices, but mostly because there's no waiting.

The other week I patronized a restaurant advertising a buy-one-get-one-half-price meat special — anything with meat in it, you could get two of, and pay half price for the least expensive dish. Lured by this attractive offer, I entered the establishment and settled myself into a booth.

I sat there unattended for at least ten minutes, feeling like an idiot. All I wanted was a menu, to peruse the different types of available meat. A beverage would've been nice. Who doesn't want a beverage? Finally I went up to the bar myself and requested a Sprite.

When I returned to my booth, there was a menu on the table as if it had been magically delivered by sprites, by which I mean the elusive, supernatural elf or fairy kind, not what I was drinking, which wouldn't make any sense at all.

A waitress came by several more minutes later to take my order. She was pleasant enough, but I couldn't look her in the eye due to my preoccupation with thinking how she must have seen me sitting in my booth for so long with nobody coming over, including herself.

Then I sat and waited for my food.

At one point the waitress came by again to ask if I wanted another Sprite, and I said no and then because she looked like a nice person who was also curious about the world, I asked her, "Why do they make ketchup bottles red now?"

She seemed confused, so I picked up the red ketchup bottle on the table to give her a good look at it. I said, "Do you remember when the bottles used to be clear, and you could see how much ketchup was left inside? Now there's no way of knowing. I'm looking at this ketchup bottle and I'm thinking, *Will there be enough ketchup in here for my beef brisket and my turkey drumsticks when they arrive?* That's a nagging doubt I'd prefer not to have. You can sort of tell by the weight of the bottle, I suppose. I could give it a shake and guesstimate the contents that way. But maybe I don't want to. Maybe I like to be sure."

"So no drink, then?" she said.

"No thanks," I said.

She walked away, and eventually returned with my meal. In the end, I left an okay tip but not a great tip, on account of the initial awkward Sprite situation.

So I went back to our exclusive nook with my dumpling and my salad selections, having arranged the beets — of course — on the bottom, and I sat between Aunt Bernice and her daughter Ashley, who I guess technically would be my cousin, you'd think that, but not actually, seeing as Aunt Bernice is in fact a family friend and I only call her Aunt Bernice. Meaning she's not a real aunt. So the cousin thing doesn't extend to her kids — they're just Aunt Bernice's kids. Uncle Troy is Aunt Bernice's ex-husband but their divorce was amicable, so I still call him Uncle Troy because that's always been his name.

I was invited to be the usher-slash-bouncer at Ashley's wedding last month, and it was open bar for family, cash bar for everybody else. The family all wore name tags, that's how the bartenders could tell. So I didn't have a name tag but I said to the bartender, "The bride's mother is my Aunt Bernice." And the bartender said, "So the bride is your cousin?" I said, "No, to me she's just Aunt Bernice's kid." And he said, "Four-fifty."

Aunt Bernice had a major pile of fried rice on her plate.

To make some friendly conversation, I said to her, "You like that fried rice, Aunt Bernice?"

She pointed a chopstick at me and sort of twirled it in the air as if to make a delicate light painting. "What do you think,

Glenn? I went and served myself all this fried rice because I hate fried rice? Yeah, fried rice makes me want to puke, so I made sure to get a lot of it."

I was pretty sure she was being sarcastic, so I laughed, and then I told her she should be careful because the other day I was eating an apricot and it crunched instead of squished, which meant there was a fragment of a pit left inside. I almost broke my tooth on it.

"Poor you," said Aunt Bernice.

"Thanks," I said, "but don't worry, I was okay. I'm just telling you as more of a cautionary tale because people break their teeth on hidden hard things all the time. Even with rice you have to be careful. There could be a pebble in there and you wouldn't even know it. Just chew slowly. I can rake through it with my fork if you want."

"Keep your goddamn fork to yourself," she said.

I turned to Ashley on my other side and laughed, "Oh boy, that mother of yours!"

Ashley frowned. Her small features were concentrated in the middle of her face, so her frown had the effect of compressing them nearly into oblivion. "What about her?"

I said, "Nothing," and cut open my dumpling. At which point I almost puked due to the pinkness inside, which was unexpected.

Ashley's husband Stefano was sitting across from me and saw the whole thing, so I said to him, "Lucky for me I cut into this first — it's pink! Move along, salmonella, I won't be making your unpleasant acquaintance tonight."

He said, "It's shrimp. Shrimp's supposed to be pink."

I said, "Oh."

At the wedding reception, Stefano was drinking heavily and I had to take him outside for some air at one point. He was ranting and raving about his job and how much he hated it but how he couldn't quit because Ashley had trapped him because she wanted to have a baby someday, so there was no way he could quit his horrible job now that they were going to be responsible for a child in the future.

To calm him down I told him about a video I'd watched on YouTube involving monkeys that had really affected me. There were these two cute little grey monkeys in two cages beside each other. They were in a lab, and a scientist explained that each monkey would be expected to perform the same task of handing him a wood chip from the pile in front of them. However, they would each receive different rewards — one monkey would get a grape, and the other monkey would get a piece of cucumber. The idea was to demonstrate that even animals become upset when they don't get equal pay for equal work.

I told Stefano I could certainly relate to that, because recently my wages had been slashed due to cutbacks at the newspaper, and yet I was still categorizing the exact same number of classified ads as before, so how was that fair?

When the second monkey got his first cucumber piece, he didn't seem to mind, and gobbled it up. But when he watched his neighbour get the grape, he did his task twice as quickly the next time, and then sat there waiting for his grape. When he got more cucumber instead, he went nuts. He threw the cucumber piece and all the woodchips out of his cage. He hooted with indignation. He flailed his long arm through the bars in search of something, anything, to destroy.

I told Stefano that I felt so sorry for that poor creature in this dumb experiment to prove a hypothesis that was already basic common knowledge. *Just give Number Two a grape already!* I wanted to scream at the scientist. *He's doing a good job!* All I wanted to do was take that enraged monkey in my arms and feed it grape after grape until it was full to bursting.

At that point, Aunt Bernice's new son-in-law took a swing at me, so I had to put the groom in a choke hold until the fight went out of him.

That memory reminded me of how I'd also promised Uncle Troy that nobody in our group would die from asphyxiation, so I went over the steps for the Heimlich manoeuvre to keep them fresh in my brain, just in case.

That's when this guy who I didn't recognize stuck his head around the decorative folding screen that was acting as a graceful and effective partition against the prying eyes of other diners.

I shouted, "Private party!" And the guy went away.

"Attaboy, Glenn-o!" Uncle Troy yelled from over by the stunning wall-mounted display of samurai swords entwined with plastic orchids.

I yelled back, "I'm your man, Uncle Troy!" And I pretend-saluted him again, then stood and made my way back to the food area because it was time for Round Number Two.

I wasn't concerned about eating too much and feeling

uncomfortably stuffed. I knew I was going to walk home later, because I'd already asked if anyone had room in their car for me but nobody did. But that was okay because it's easy to eat too much food at a buffet, so it would be good to get some exercise afterwards.

I'd taken a bus to the restaurant and I didn't mind that either. I always enjoy public transit because I like listening to people talking on their cellphones. They share touching or hilarious anecdotes about their personal lives, or they ask each other if they've seen any good movies lately and then smile at the other person's response. They say they miss each other, and they lean into their phones and press their ear up against the speaker. Once I heard an older woman telling whoever was on the other line, "There might be a storm tonight but don't worry. Even if you hear thunder. I know that's a sound you don't like, but don't worry about it, because thunder is just a loud noise and it can't hurt you. Even if it sounds scary." That was one of my favourites.

I grabbed a new plate and visited the chow mein station and started scooping, and this guy on my left said, "Looks like it's a private party for that chow mein."

I glanced at him, kind of over my shoulder. "You got a problem, pal?"

That's when I realized it was the same guy who'd stuck his head into our room a few minutes prior.

"I didn't have any problems until I met you," he said.

I said, "I don't want any trouble here. It's Dumpling Night."

He asked me, "You tried the shrimp kind?"

I shook my head. "I thought it was something else."

"Shrimp's like that," he said. "Always masquerading."

And I knew he was having a go at me there because since when is a shrimp anything but a shrimp? Since never, that's when.

By this time, a crowd had gathered. But not because they wanted to see the two of us come to blows — more because they wanted chow mein.

"Are you going to stand there all day, or move, or what?" grumbled a lady in the long line-up of people keen on getting some mouth-watering bean-sprout hash before they expired from a bean-sprout deficiency.

So I stepped aside and the guy stepped aside and the crowd progressed along the table, shovelling and scraping.

Then the guy said to me, "I was looking in that room for my Aunt Bernice. You didn't have to yell at me like that."

"Your Aunt Bernice?" I said. "I've got an Aunt Bernice!"

"Oh yeah?" The guy squinted at my face. "You don't look like you're related."

"She's not my blood aunt," I said. "She's more like my aunt by my parents' marriage. They're friends."

"Huh," said the guy. "Well, she's really my real, actual aunt."

"So you're Aunt Bernice's nephew. How about that?" I said. "And here I thought I'd met all the relations at Ashley's wedding last month."

"I had other plans that day. Who are you, again?"

"A very close family friend."

He nodded, and the two of us stood there for a moment, kind of mesmerized by each other is I suppose what the situation was.

Then the guy said, "I guess I'd better get in there."

"Yep," I said. "You'd better."

As a gesture of our newfound fraternity, Aunt Bernice's nephew tipped his plate in my direction, but only very slightly since there were some chicken balls rolling around on it.

Then he walked over to that private room and disappeared into its glittery depths as a fish might fling itself into a beautiful ornamental pond.

I turned and headed back to the dumpling table, partly because I wanted more dumplings, but mostly because right then I couldn't think of anywhere else to go.

# THINGS NOT TO DO

I AM THE TYPE of person who gets very annoyed at the type of people who don't pay attention.

As a human being living on a planet with other human beings — as well as flora and fauna and inanimate objects and bugs, et cetera — my feeling is, you should have a basic sense of the space you take up in the world, and at least a general idea of who is occupying the space around you.

Essentially all I'm saying is, just be aware, okay?

Awareness is your responsibility as a social animal. If you're on a crowded sidewalk, please, whatever you do, do not stop suddenly in the middle of it to check your phone. Because, as you should realize, there are myriad souls diligently traversing an assortment of distances behind you, and if you cease your own movement, they will by default have to cease theirs. That's just simple physics. Which admittedly I know very little about, and I might have Googled *How does physics apply* to this or that situation at various times in my life on various quests to prove a point with more than just anecdotal evidence once in a while, but in any case, "That's just simple physics" is a true statement, at least in this instance.

Because normal people understand that causing hindrance in the lives of others is unacceptable, always.

My husband says I get too worked up about this stuff.

I say he's wrong.

We were at the airport once, coming home from somewhere, I don't know, the location in this narrative isn't important, though I will concede that yes, setting does play a vital role in conjuring up a better picture of a scenario. So let's say we had just flown home from Fiji. Because I have always wanted to go to Fiji. So obviously what I've just admitted is that we were not flying home from Fiji. But that's entirely beside the point.

So we've got all our bags, after obtaining them in the correct way, which, as every normal person with a functioning brain knows, involves extending respect to your fellow exhausted travellers by resisting the nearly irresistible — and okay yes, tantalizing — urge to yank a suitcase that you are quite sure is not your own, but that resembles your own, off the carousel, then proceed to turn it around and around as you search in vain for the identifying googog that you'd handily attached to your own luggage for quick and easy identification. So, bingo, where is the googog? Not here. Okay, heave the suitcase back into rotation, because that's definitely not it.

Obviously, that sort of behaviour slows everyone down.

And we were bone-weary and once giddy with too many tiny bottles of Riesling but no longer, as the giddiness had been replaced by headaches, followed by anger. We had all of our bags, and all we wanted was to flash our customs form at the customs officer and have him or her wave us through the sliding doors. Because even though you know you've done nothing wrong, there is always that anxiety that the uniformed arm will point you in the wrong direction. *Are they going to direct us down the hall? Are they going to direct us down the hall?* And then the additional anxiety on top of that, about whatever it is you might be anxious about a stranger discovering, and then judging you for, and then noting that discovery in a file for the government, which will never, ever be erased. *I do not want them to find the sadomasochistic erotica I purchased abroad. I do not want them to find the sadomasochistic erotica I purchased abroad.* That sort of anxiety.

So we had our bags, and we displayed our customs form proudly and openly as befitted innocent civilians with nothing to hide, and then — *thank God thank God thank Christ because that would have been embarrassing and there are some other things in there too, now that I think about it, Jesus, just imagine* — the sliding doors parted and we were free and blameless and finally on our way home.

And then a woman stopped in front of us.

Came to a complete, dead stop on the exit ramp with her giant suitcase, one of those absurdly large hard-case ones that you see and you think, *Really? Do you have an actual need for a suitcase that big? You couldn't have left a few of your precious belongings at home? You had to bring absolutely every single thing that you own with you on your week-long vacation? Of course you did. Because you always have to be comfortable, and discomfort is anathema to you.*

*Because you are weak.*

She stopped because she had spotted somebody she knew, someone who was there to pick her up or reunite with her or what have you. I don't know, her mother or whoever. And she wanted to hug that person.

So there she was, directly in front of us, hugging, and I cleared my throat as loudly as possible to do her the favour of first offering this unspoken directive, to spare her the humiliation of a vocal public shaming, to instead wordlessly communicate the necessity for her to *Move, move now, get out of the way, you are creating a traffic jam of flesh, and people have to physically move around you now, because you are in the way.*

But she didn't move. She only kept hugging, and obstructing.

So I pushed her.

I didn't push her over. I merely pushed past her. More forcefully than I probably should have, okay. But I was impatient, and with that force I exerted I was also expressing the amalgamated impatience of every other bedraggled, jet-lagged globetrotter whose paths she was barricading. I drew strength from that communal wellspring of resentment. And I used my elbows a little, which my husband later said was cruel, but he can't even watch the torture scenes on 24 so I have to describe what's happening while he sits there with his eyes closed. Because even though he's squeamish about the fingernail-pulling or electrical-cable-whipping or power-drill-applying or whatever, he doesn't want to miss any of the action. And then he'll turn around and want me to call him Jack Bauer during our lovemaking, and I do, because I love him, but I'm always thinking, *Jack Bauer has more manhood in his baby toe than you have in your entire, overly hairy and too-soft body*.

So with that, we continued on, unfettered no more by ignorance and insensitivity.

And then my husband said to me, "You were kind of being a bitch back there, Angie."

In that instant, I had to grapple with my own hideously antisocial compulsion to disrupt the smooth passage of the other members of our throng, because I very much wanted to halt my progress through the arrivals area and point a finger at my husband's stupidly trembling chin and flaring nostrils. But I am a considerate and thoughtful person, so instead I kept moving and asked him, "What did you just say to me, Robert?"

And he said, "Just the whole thing back there. It was kind of unnecessary, don't you think? That lady didn't block our way on purpose. She probably didn't even know we were behind her."

And I said, "Robert, don't you think that's a problem? For a person in an airport — which is, by its very nature, a terminus for multitudes — to be so completely and utterly unaware of her surroundings?"

To which he replied, quietly, "She was hugging her mother, for God's sake."

And I said, "Robert, she is in a very busy place. She is one of thousands who have lives to live and loved ones to greet. Okay, sure, embrace your mother. But first step to the side, by God.

Step to the side, and do not just stand there and make everybody else go around you."

Robert said something else then, I don't remember what, and I ignored him.

And we proceeded to the parking lot, and we found our car and filled the trunk with our regular-sized suitcases, and we drove home.

Then we went directly to our bedroom and unpacked our suitcases, and we put the dirty clothes into the laundry hamper and we put the clean clothes away in their proper places.

Then we brushed our teeth and washed our faces and applied moisturizer judiciously and changed into the fresh sets of pajamas we had laid out before our trip to welcome us upon our return.

Finally, we climbed into bed and pulled the covers up to our necks, and revelled in our apportioned sections of mattress before falling asleep almost immediately. At which point I dreamed about vast expanses of beautifully unobstructed exit ramps with a glorious abundance of unlimited space for everyone to use and enjoy.

Because those, right there, are the things that normal people do.

# HE WILL SPEAK TO US

THE GIRLS ARE SCREAMING, like always. There's thousands of them and they're loud in that way only teenage girls can be loud. And Jesus, he's not even on the screen yet.

His music's playing in advance of the big speech, though, so the girls are all dancing in ways that teenage girls really shouldn't be dancing. Rubbing up against each other and shoving their hands into their crazy hair.

Some of them stay posed like that for a while, up to their wrists in spikes and curls and feathers and lace, with their pointy elbows splayed out and the super-soft skin of their inner arms exposed. Like their fingers are stuck and there's an animal in there, biting. It must be a new sort of dance because a bunch of them are doing it.

I go to the bar and order a couple of beers. The bartender smiles wide and tells me I look familiar. I get this a lot. I could lay on the suspense, but I don't because I'm not a dick that way.

I tell him who I am, and wait for him to tell me the beers are on the house.

"Dude, I knew it!" He takes two cans out of the fridge and pops them open. They hiss as foam pushes out and slides down the sides. "That'll be twelve bucks."

I wink at the guy. "Come on."

"Sorry, bud." He shrugs, then grins over at the huge blank screen at the front of the concert hall. "So I'd ask if you were all proud and shit, but then, you know…"

People are like this. They want you to just come out and say what they want to hear. Like you owe them some sort of explanation. Like it's my fault he turned out the way he did. They want it all up front for free, my rotten guts exposed to the harsh rays of their holier-than-thou judgment. I don't say a word.

"So he's giving the big speech tonight. You help him with that? Coach him or whatever?"

"Not me," I say. "Excuses are his mother's department."

"That's funny." He drums his hands against the sides of his cash register. "That's a good one. So's he going to sing for us after?"

"How the hell am I supposed to know?" I take some bills out of my wallet and flash him my son's picture while I'm at it, because I'm the kind of dad who keeps a photo of his son in his wallet. Something most people don't know about me.

A FEW MONTHS AGO, when he was filming a music video in Philadelphia, I sent him a poem. The poem first came to me in a forward from my buddy Terry's wife Stephanie. Usually I hate forwards and the people who send them. But Stephanie always packs leftovers for Terry to bring me when he comes over, so I can't hate her, even though at the bottom of her emails there's a cartoon squirrel with a speech bubble that says, *The whole world's gone nuts!!!*

This particular forward from Stephanie was so supremely positive that I printed it out right away, squirrel and all, and mailed it to my son. The poem was about how it's actually hurting other people if you don't let your own inner light shine as brightly as possible. If you dull your luminosity, which was previously helping to guide the way for others who are going along their own mediocre paths in life, then those other people will be plunged into a terrifying blackness, and may even be harmed or killed by snakes or lizards or predatory giant cats, and it will be your fault because you turned out your own light and let the darkness in.

His reply to my poem, which I'd mailed to him in all sincerity, was a postcard, and the only thing he wrote on the card was, *Remember how you used to spread cream cheese on my bagel?* Like he was giving me a pop quiz.

Of course I remembered the cream cheese. I used to spread it extra-thick, so much that the cheese layer was almost the thickness of the bagel half. He didn't mention the raisins, though, and that bugged me.

I used to drop a few raisins on top of the cream cheese, and I'd give him the bagel and go, "Oh no, a bunny crapped on your breakfast!" It always made him laugh. Or most times, anyway. He was a hard kid to make laugh. He went around looking serious all the time, like he had this special purpose in life or something.

So he remembers the cream cheese part, but not the raisins, which was the comedy gold element of the whole exchange. Or maybe this is more of a selective memory issue we're dealing with here. Because to me, it was like he deliberately left that part out.

There is no possible way he could've forgotten about the raisins.

I TAKE THE BEERS over to Terry, who's chatting up some girl who looks about twelve under all the goop that's supposed to make her look older and more experienced. I hand Terry his can and introduce myself to her, and she squeals, like I was expecting.

She grabs my arm and I feel her fingers squeezing like a grabby fish. "Oh my God!" she says. "Did you, like, help him write his speech for tonight and everything?"

"I might've had a hand in it." I flex my bicep, which is pretty decent, under her skinny fingers. "And maybe my hand was holding a pen, is all I'm going to speak to that subject."

She trembles like a baby raccoon when you shine a flashlight in its face. "Ohhh, I love him, he's so nice!" she says, and her eyes roll back in her head a bit, showing the whites. "He is such a nice person!"

Terry is hopping from one foot to another, kind of weirdly dancing in place and eyeing this girl up.

I shoot him a look like, *Come on, guy, she probably hasn't even had her period yet.* I grab his beer to wake him up, and take a big slug and he goes, "Hey!"

The girl giggles. "I'm too young to drink beer, see?" And she holds out her bony little wrist that either one of us could take and snap clean in half with barely any effort. She shows us the yellow band that the powers-that-be made her wear, and all the other girls too, so the moron bartender knows not to serve them.

I reflect that one of the perks of being a VIP is they let you in through a special back door, and instead of patting you down they say, "Good evening, sir." I hand my beer to Terry and take out my pocket knife.

The girl's eyes go wide and I snip the band off her. I kick it away into the shuffling rainbow of sneakers encircling us, and say to her, "We don't need people telling us what we can and can't do around here, do we?"

She laughs in a fast, high burst, and throws back her head so I can see right inside her pretty pink mouth, with all her teeth lined up perfectly white, not a bit of silver in any of them. But then I guess fillings are clear nowadays, so maybe she has a whole mouthful of cavities. Maybe she's been gobbling candy her whole short life like the bad little girl she is.

ANOTHER LITTLE-KNOWN FACT about me is that after his mom and I broke up, I was the one who got custody. His mom went and screwed off to Tahiti — she got a cruise-ship job that she thought would make her an international star, because she would be performing in various parts of the world and people from different countries were going to see her onstage. But she was just one member of this giant cast that sang covers of hits from the seventies, so what really did she think was going to happen?

He and I had our own thing going. I purchased this discounted medium-tame bobcat from an exotic pet dealer who was going out of business. The cat was really old and had arthritis pretty bad, but it was still very impressive, wild-animal-wise.

The three of us took the show on the road, with me of course in the management role, and the bobcat would do tricks. And my son would sing — just covers at first, but then it was songs he invented on his own. People fucking loved us.

I SAY, "TERRY, GO get us more beers, will you?"

He frowns at me but goes to the bar. Because he knows he wouldn't be here, with so many body piercings on display, sparkling at us, if it wasn't for me.

The girl is staring at the screen all intense and fixated, like she's psychically willing my son to appear. Her fists are clenching open and closed and I want to stick my finger in there, see how strong her grip is.

I say, "What did you think when you heard about what he did?"

"Who, me?" She giggles. "I don't know."

"What about your friends?"

"They're over there somewhere."

Thousands of young female heads are facing the screen, like sunflowers swivelling towards the sun. This is an interesting fact that he and I learned together years ago, in a field of them. Sunflowers literally turn their stalks around in the dirt. Or maybe that's not even true, who knows. But it's neat to think about. We had a shared curiosity about the natural world, the two of us.

HE USED TO ASK me stupid questions all the time. He always tried to see how far he could push me. He'd say, "Do you love me?" And I'd say, "Of course I love you. I'm your dad."

"But what if we were strangers and we saw each other across a crowded room? Would you walk over to my side and introduce yourself? Would you want to meet me? And what if Christopher was in the room too — would you go over to him first, or me?"

Christopher was my name for the bobcat because that was what I wanted to call my son when he was born. But his mother had her own ideas, and that was back when I could still be charmed by her feminine wiliness, so let's suffice it to say she won that war.

This was way before anybody knew who he was. He was just a boy with a nice voice. And when we got booked for the birthday parties and bachelorettes and bar mitzvahs, lots of times the host would say to me, "The kid doesn't have to sing, it's okay, we just want to pet the bobcat." So everybody would swarm around Christopher and get their picture taken at an additional cost, and meanwhile my son would be standing around doing nothing.

Eventually he'd get bored and bat his eyelashes at the lady of the house, tell her stories about how he was going to be famous someday. Then he'd ask her to make him a sandwich, giving off the appearance that I didn't feed him, like he was starving or something, from abuse or neglect or whatever. He was a little liar even back then.

I SAY TO THE girl, "Do your parents know about this, or is it a secret?" And I give her little bejewelled belly ring the lightest tap, barely even touching it at all, but feeling some skin still. Her face goes pale under the makeup, and she winces. "Don't do that."

"Shit, sorry," I say, and put my hands in my pockets.

"I wouldn't mind, normally." She sticks a chunk of glittery hair in her mouth, sucks on it hard. "Only because it's infected."

I bend down for a closer look. The flesh around the ring is puffed up, devil-red. It must hurt like a bitch.

SO THEN HIS MOTHER suddenly wants him back in her life. She's all saved and reborn after she met this evangelist on the cruise ship. She said the evangelist told her she had more talent in the tiny nail on her baby toe than the rest of the cast had in their whole bodies. Now that's a line if I ever heard one, because she was just up there kicking her legs and shaking her ass with all the other similar legs and asses. How could she possibly stand out from the crowd like he said she did?

But she went back to the evangelist's stateroom with an ocean view, and apparently it was magical. And then presto, they're together in his huge RV with a bunch of animals, but domesticated, not like our amazing bobcat, which was dead by this point. It died in its sleep. The next morning my son comes running into my room, shaking and crying hysterically, "Christopher is hard like a stone, he's not moving, he's not breathing." He had a flair for performance from the very beginning.

TERRY COMES BACK WITH three beers. I say, "What do you think you're doing?"

He says, "You're the one who cut her tag off."

The girl eyes the silver can he's dangling, then eyes me. "Please?"

I look around. Shrieking underage girls are cocooning us in from all sides. We're the only adults in sight.

She says, "I won't tell anybody."

HIS MOTHER CALLS ME up one day from the evangelist's motor home, which was her motor home now too, and she says, "We want him back." And I go, "Who is we?" Then she proceeds to tell me the story about the cruise ship and her talented toe and the magical night, and what, so now they're a family and all they need to complete the picture is a kid?

She said our son's God-given musical gift was languishing under my guardianship. She said she and her evangelist boyfriend were uniquely positioned to bestow upon him the brightest possible future, what with their combined backgrounds in the entertainment and religious industries.

I said, "Whoa, big words for a small-time cover-tune dancer."

But, to be honest, I didn't put up much of a fight because by that point I was tired, I was worn out from Christopher's death. Truth be told, I was ready to start dating again myself, but it was hard to meet anybody because I couldn't get out to the bars. Or at least I couldn't stay at them very late because I didn't want to leave him alone in a motel room for very long by himself. Even though I always paid the front-desk guys a few bucks to check in on him every half hour, make sure he was still breathing and hadn't been snatched up by some pervert.

TERRY GOES TO TAKE a piss, and when he's gone, the music cuts out and the crowd quiets right down. Except they're still whispering to each other or going, "Shhh!" So the massive room is filled with an ear-splintering hush.

The screen stays blank, though. Then the announcer's voice booms out of the speakers, "Ladies! Your favourite pop star in the whole entire universe will be with us momentarily. Only a few more minutes now!" And the crowd sucks in one breath all at once, and lets it out in one giant scream.

Because it's so loud, the girl stands up on her tiptoes and presses her mouth against my ear. She says, "Tell me something about him." Then she takes a step back and does a slow, shimmying dance, just for me.

I don't hesitate. "His favourite food is chocolate chip banana bread."

She squishes up her face like somebody let one rip. "I already know that! It's on his website, silly."

I've been tossing around this idea lately for my own website, involving the displaying and selling of his memorabilia, stuff I kept from when he was a kid. But I didn't keep very much, so I probably won't bother.

The girl grabs my arm again, her nails digging in. "Tell me something about him that only his family knows. Tell me something personal."

WHEN THE LASER TAG incident happened, it's important to note that he was in his mother's custody. I thought about calling her up and asking what happened to discipline, what happened to manners? But I didn't really give a shit. She and the evangelist might have cooked up the whole thing for all I knew, just another publicity stunt that in theory would've catapulted him to even more superstardom but in practice ended up going shittily for everyone involved.

The story is that he assaulted a non-famous kid in the special combat room at SensorDome. He told the papers, "It was really dark in there, even with the lasers. And he was coming at me with what appeared to be pure malice, so I had to defend myself."

From the hospital, the non-famous kid kept saying to the reporters what a treat it had been to meet his musical hero, and how tall and commanding he was in person, as in an actual one-on-one, face-to-face exchange.

But then the non-famous kid went and died from internal injuries, and suddenly I'm getting calls for interviews all over the place, and I'm booked up with speaking engagements at elementary schools because apparently now I'm the resident expert on parenting a troubled preteen. They want to know what they can do better than me, is basically it. And then I get a personal VIP invitation-with-guest-optional for tonight. Terry was all, "Take me, take me!" I said to him, "Who else do I have, idiot?"

To top it off, some asshole reporter stopped me on the street last week and asked me did I think raising my son alongside a wild jungle feline somehow contributed to his delinquency, his lack of empathy, his complete disregard for his fellow human beings?

I said first off, bobcats live in forests, and second, maybe it did play a factor in his upbringing, but all I could say with full and absolute certainty was that in my custodial care, my son was fed and clothed and housed. And even though we moved around a lot, he and Christopher were like brothers, and he would rub his face in Christopher's whiskers and that cat would purr and purr. And if anything, I learned a thing or two from the kid and his generosity of spirit, his angelic voice from straight out of heaven.

I said as far as I was concerned, the laser tag killing was manslaughter, if anything. It was definitely not a premeditated act. It couldn't have been, because he doesn't have the soul of a murderer inside of him. Otherwise I, as his father who knows him, would've seen it curling out of his nose and ears like a spiteful grey spectre of badness. And okay, maybe there was that time when he took my toenail clippers and snipped off the end of Christopher's tail, which I hear is the most sensitive part. And occasionally he would punch Christopher in the head just to make him yowl. Okay, there was that.

But ultimately — and I think though the real-life jury may be out on this, the figurative jury would be in absolute total agreement — he was put on this green Earth to entertain, to teach us all about our better natures, and at no time did he ever express to me the desire to enact a bloodlust upon his fellow men, women, or children.

TERRY'S HEAD IS COMING at us through the crowd. We're both taller than everybody else here, so I spot him easy. He's maybe ten minutes away though, because of how packed-in the audience is. I've still got time.

I wrap my arm around the girl's waist and pull her close. I tell her, "We used to rake the leaves together.

"We rounded them up into neat, multi-coloured piles, as subdued and graceful as his mother was when she came outside in the crisp autumn air and brought us snacks on a plate decorated with a paper doily. Then we turned our backs to the piles for a few seconds, satisfied with our labours. We clapped each other on the shoulders for being such an unstoppable father-and-son team. We let our rakes fall, and when they nearly sliced off our feet, we jumped back just in time and congratulated each other on our agility.

"But when we turned back around to admire our handiwork, the leaf piles had changed. They pulsed, and the colour had bled out of them so now they were a muddy grey-brown. We still wanted to jump in. We wanted to so badly — we were desperate with the need to ruin everything we had accomplished. Roll all over it, bulldoze it, make those leaves fly and then crush them.

"When we couldn't resist any longer, we held our breath and bent our knees and leaped, and we were in! But things were not what we had expected. We were surrounded on all sides. Instead of succumbing to our combined brute force, the rotting leaves closed in, smothering us. It was dark in there, and wet, or damp in the areas that hadn't yet fully committed to being wet. Not a good place to be. But we had only ourselves to blame. We had gone about the chore diligently, and the leaves had followed our instructions, lining up with heads bowed. But they were only biding their time, waiting for the right moment.

"We became unsure of ourselves and the path we wanted to take. We'd known it a split second ago — were absolutely and unshakably sure. But now we didn't know which end was up, where the sky was or where the ground was. And we lost each other."

The screen flickers then and the music stops, and the noise goes out of the crowd, whoosh.

The girl shakes my arm loose and backs away from me, disappears into the hot press of moist smoothness and ripped tights and dollar-store tiaras and clattering strings of Mardi Gras-type beads, which these young ladies don't even understand the true meaning of.

I look around for Terry but don't see his head anymore, and I figure that means either he's fallen or he's lying down somewhere on purpose.

Everybody is jostling hard, a dose of the scary strength and sharpness of endless prepubescent female knees and elbows. Girls shove past me from every possible angle, shove each other too and pull hair, surging forward and blocking each other out. Wanting him all to themselves.

I move to the back and stand my ground, and stare with everybody else as the giant screen fills with my son's beautiful face. And wait with everybody else to hear him say he's sorry.

# EVERYONE HERE IS SO FRIENDLY

YOU MEET A NEW friend and he tells you you're the best guy he's ever known.

You say, "Hey, maybe I'm not the best guy."

"No," he says. "You are."

"Okay," you say.

NOW YOU AND YOUR friend are on tour, and all you do is visit different cities and go to parties together and that's cool because when you were in high school, all of your peers went to parties every weekend or else rock 'n' bowl but you were never invited. But that's okay because you were too busy babysitting.

Once you looked after some kids and they made you play Dog, which meant that you had to get down on all fours, and the kids tied a skipping rope around your neck. They yanked on the rope and yelled, "Bark!" You coughed because the rope was too tight, and they said you had to be punished and go in the doghouse, also known as their parents' closet. You wanted these kids to get the best possible start in life so you crawled in, and they locked the door. You sat back on your haunches, whimpered. They were going to get a bad report for this. You tried to make them behave so they would get a good report, but now that wasn't possible.

You also had a job folding shirts at a store. That kept you busy too.

YOU AND YOUR FRIEND visit another city and go to another party, and right away you get the sense it's going to be a real smasheroo. People are jumping up and down, spilling drinks, giving each other makeovers.

The room is big and white with twinkling lights everywhere, and when the hostess swishes over to greet you, she explains that the idea is for the guests to feel as if they have just escaped from a miserable totalitarian regime.

The hostess is sparkly all over because of the sparkles on her tight dress and she's got sparkles on her pretty face as well. You want to ask her did she get those sparkles from Heaven? Because you believe in Heaven, very much. But you think, *Be cool, be cool*. Because your friend has been teaching you how to act around women and one of the things you're not supposed to do is be whimsical.

So instead you tell her that's a stupid theme for a party and you say something negative about her appearance to make her cry.

Your friend gives you the thumbs-up, and the two of you begin to hobnob.

THE EVENING GETS DARKER and all the guests look familiar, as if they could be your cousins, only nicer. As soon as your friend tells them your name, they gasp with delight and applaud with enthusiasm.

You're still not used to this kind of treatment. At home, your cousins pushed you down and kicked you and called you mean names like "Wiglet."

You and your friend engage in conversation with some partygoers.

They say, "Wow, you two seem pretty close."

You tell them that when you and your friend go for walks together, he doesn't play the trick that other people used to play on you, where they waited until you were looking in the opposite direction and then they'd run off and hide.

Your friend mock-punches you in the arm with one of his large, manly hands and asks, "Are you having a good time?"

You say, "Yes, but I'm disappointed I didn't get to blow up any balloons."

He summons a pink, wrinkly lady who is hunched under her tray of miniature crab cakes, and whispers in her ear. She makes her thumb and forefinger into a gun and blows on it like it's smoking. She puts down her tray and scurries to a closet and emerges with a pink, wrinkly balloon that is yours to personally inflate.

It's a relief to be part of the action because the party is a potluck but nobody told you, so you didn't bring anything to contribute. You feel like a fool, showing up empty-handed.

Your friend says, "It's okay, they already have too much

potato salad, anyway."

You say, "Whoa, how did you know I was going to bring potato salad?"

He winks. "I know all your secrets."

You blush the shade of pink that people at home used to say was the colour of canned ham.

But here your friend places his big, hot palms on your quivering shoulders and says, "Your secrets are beautiful, and so are you."

AT HOME, YOU HAD nightmares about the end of the world. A tsunami, a cyclone. You tried to rally everyone to flee the city, or take shelter in a basement. A few of them listened to you at first, but then your cousins pushed you down and kicked you and said, "Who do you think you are?" and nobody listened after that. You couldn't even command attention when the world was ending.

And it's a funny story how you met your friend. It was during a terrible storm and you were running down the sidewalk in the rain, looking for shelter. Then you stumbled into a dark bar that ended up being full of light, because the man who would quickly become your closest confidant, staunchest supporter, and all-around best buddy was in there.

He gave you the shelter you were seeking, although you didn't realize that at the time. You didn't realize it until later, when he told you.

YOUR FRIEND SAYS HE has to do some business dealings with a man on the other side of the room who sells goldfish or robots or maybe robot guns that shoot goldfish? You're not sure about the last part because his mouth was full when he was telling you, which was really gross but you let it slide because he's your friend.

You ask if you can come too but he says, "Nah, you just enjoy yourself."

He walks away to work his magic, and you go and stand beside the chips-and-dip table.

You eat some chips and dip.

YOU ARE AN INTERNATIONALLY renowned YouTube sensation, and it's all because of your friend.

Nobody else saw the talent shining from way down deep inside you, but he did.

He told you he saw it immediately, when you sat down next to him at the bar and apologized for your coat dripping all over his shoes. He said don't worry about it, and you bought him a beer for being so understanding. In the process, you were embarrassed to find that your wallet was soaked too, and when you withdrew it from your pocket, you accidentally sprayed more rain droplets on the stranger. But he said it was no prob-lem at all, which was so kind of him, and when you laid all your cards out to dry by the shiny brass taps, you saw your reflection there, and it was smiling.

Evidently, the feeling was mutual, because your friend later told you that when he met you, he was blinded and uplifted all at once. He said it was as if he was a homeless person and you'd just kicked him awake, shone a flashlight in his eyes, and given him a delicious slice of hot, gooey pizza. In reality you would never do that to a homeless person, or anybody, because it would be cruel. But it's still a neat idea to think about.

A BUNCH OF GUESTS run over and take selfies with you, without even asking, right at the moment when your cheeks are unattractively bulging with hors d'oeuvres.

You want to spit your chewed-up food in their faces, but you don't, because your friend has been teaching you that being humble doesn't matter, but appearing humble does.

The guests lose interest in you once they've shared all their photos, and a space opens around you like a powerful force field.

Across the room, your friend mock-punches the businessman on the arm, and the businessman responds by rubbing his arm in mock pain. Your friend laughs with far more exuberance than the circumstance seems to call for.

You scoop some dip with enough force to break the chip. You leave the broken-off part to soften and disintegrate in the bowl.

A boring guy comes up and asks you, "What kind of dip is that?"

"How am I supposed to know?" you say. "I'm the idiot who didn't bring anything, remember?"

The guy smiles and nods and leaves you alone again.

You overhear some dialogue that goes like this:

"It's so much freer here, don't you think?"

"Oh, I agree. Everyone here is so friendly, and open. Have you been to Vienna? The Viennese are like monsters compared to the people here."

The revellers chortle and don't pay any attention to you at all.

YOU HAD POSTED AN assortment of videos on YouTube but they only got twelve views in total, which is not a lot of views. So you figured nobody cared about your self-recorded comedy routines that pointed out the various inequities plaguing modern society, or the way you'd always finish off by deadpanning, "Awww screw it, I'd rather eat cheese!"

But when you were sitting there at the bar with your new friend and you both ran out of conversation topics, he happened to ask if you had any good YouTube videos to show him. And you said yes, a little shyly at first, but your boldness grew alongside his interest, which was incredibly keen.

As luck would have it, the bar even had a popcorn machine, and your friend insisted on filling two of the little paper bags to the brim before settling himself in front of your tiny screen. You thought he'd offer one to you but he didn't, but that was okay.

Because then, just like a real audience member, he scarfed down his salty snack and ordered more drinks and watched every single second of all of your performances.

And at the end, when you asked if he thought you were funny, he laughed so loudly and slapped his knees so hard that the bartender told him it was time to leave.

"HOORAY, HOORAY, IT'S CAKE time!" shouts the hostess, and you can't help admiring how she looks even though her lipstick is only a faint ring around her mouth now.

She asks if anybody wants to make the first cut, and you think this is maybe the most important moment of your life, but you have no idea what to do about it.

Plus you regret your choice of outfit. Everyone here is dressed informally whereas you are wearing clothes you initially thought seemed straight out of the pages of a magazine, but they stick to you in all the wrong places, and the elastic cuffs are too tight and make you feel squishy.

Your friend could've given you a heads-up about the dress code, but he didn't.

Several more hours go by. Nobody talks to you.

Meanwhile, your friend circulates among the guests and mock-punches more people on the arms. You ache for his company.

HERE'S THE REALLY EERIE part: The morning before you met your friend, you woke up and wrote in your Journal of Intentions that this year you wanted more of the kind of jingling bells that signify something significant is about to happen, or just to warn you that a cat is nearby. Because cats have that creepy way of silently sneaking up on people, and you didn't want to give them any more chances to do that to you.

Then you ate breakfast and showered and got dressed and watched some TV and ate lunch, and after that you went outside without checking the weather first. The sky was churning with dark clouds and you didn't have an umbrella, but you kept on walking anyway.

WHEN THE PARTY IS over, you're surprised to find yourself still here. It's very late and you figured you would've left by now. But if you close your eyes and concentrate, you can't even remember leaving this spot to use the toilet.

The hostess smiles at you and her sparkles aren't so sparkly anymore but she's still nice. "The guests thought you were wonderful!" she exclaims. "Would you like to take the leftovers home?"

"Sure," you say. "What the hell."

She packs a Tupperware container with pinwheel sandwiches, pigs-in-a-blanket, pita triangles that are dried out and curling up at the edges, hummus with a crust forming on top. She ties the parcel with a gold ribbon, which you appreciate, but you don't tell her you appreciate it.

You shuffle very slowly out the door, and the hostess blows you kisses and the remaining guests run over because this is their last opportunity to show you the places on their bodies where they've tattooed all of your most famous jokes.

But your friend doesn't even say goodbye.


IN THE LIMO ON the way back to your hotel, the leftovers are heavy in your lap.

You stand up and chuck them out the sunroof, and the driver whacks the steering wheel with gusto and says that's the best throw he's ever seen.

A tour bus passes by and their guide booms, "Ooh, look who we have here!"

And you wave because at home you always waved at tour

buses, to be welcoming, and maybe one confused rider would flutter his or her fingers back at you, and then your cousins would emerge from behind the bushes and attack.

But here, the entire busload waves back at you, a mass frantic flapping that must really hurt their shoulders, and you lower your hand quickly and sink back down on your cushiony seat.

To console yourself, you remember that the morning before you met your friend, you also wrote in your journal that you desired to have your situation be more like somebody else's situation, such as someone who was having a better time in life. Your next-door neighbour Kirk, for instance, who was so full of optimism. That optimism always seemed to play out in his life but never in yours, so you wanted to switch.

And now here you are, and where is Kirk?

At home with his plants, probably. Or dead.

*Yes*, you think. *Maybe Kirk is dead*.

THAT NIGHT YOU DREAM about the end of the world, and since you and your friend have more talent than anybody else, you get to be the only survivors.

Outside, the streets are full of lava.

But inside, you and your friend sit around in your sweatpants and drink beer and watch awards shows together. And in your hearts you both know that the two of you deserve to be up on a podium high-fiving each other, forever.

# EMPATHIZE OR DIE

A MAN IS WEARING a tuxedo. He is standing with his hands in his pockets, and a woman is kneeling at his feet with her arms outstretched. In place of where her head should be is a bunch of leaves blowing around, and her body is a giant high-heeled shoe, so the only actual human parts of her are those long, graceful arms. The colours are mostly grey and black and white, except for the oversized green pear floating in the sky.

Dennis shakes his head in admiration and wonders, *What is the painter trying to say about society here? Something good? Something bad?*

He is always impressed by art that makes him think. And he's in a restaurant! All he expected to do tonight was eat a hamburger. But now his cerebral gears are churning away, and what a treat it is to be inspired before he even orders his meal.

The waitress brings him a menu. She is wearing a sleeve-less top and her arms are long like the woman's in the painting over his table. Aha! He indicates the art with a dramatic flourish that is intended to be humorous and asks, "Is this a self-portrait? It's very well done."

"Are you serious?" Her laugh sounds like an angel's laugh from that movie he saw about angels that came down from Heaven to cavort with mortal men, which triggered the Apocalypse because of all the sin involved.

*Mission accomplished*, he thinks.

She says, "The owner's kid did that. Thinks he's Picasso or something. Makes me want to puke every time I see it. Can I get you a drink?"

He winks at her. "What would you recommend?"

She says, "Uh, I don't know, a coffee?"

He says, "Perfect."

Then she goes off to fulfill his wish like a mystical fairy wearing a bikini woven out of flowers and moss that she'd gathered from the enchanted forest floor. She'd had to gather a lot of flowers and moss, because she is physically gifted in the way that large-breasted women are gifted, meaning there was a lot of skin to cover. And she'd had to gather it quickly, because there were evil, lecherous goblins hiding in the woods. Meaning they would get her if she was naked.

When he opens his menu, a piece of paper flutters out in much the same way as a leaf would do in a similar situation, delightfully perpetuating the forest motif he's conjured. It says, *Open Mic Poetry Night: Tonight!*

He had no idea. All he wanted was a burger.

DENNIS HAS ALWAYS HAD a strong imagination. When he was only a boy, he used to draw a whole other menu on the paper placemats they gave out at Swiss Chalet. He drew chicken drumsticks with legs and eyes and claws, and his mom would say, "Yum! I'd like one of those, please!" She'd show his work to the waitresses and they would recoil a bit but then say, "Oh, isn't that cute." His mom would nod and tell them that he was going to be rich and famous someday, and the waitresses would smile and smile.

Then he learned how to spell, and fell in love with the alphabet. He made up lists of words he liked purely because of how they sounded. His favourite word of all time was "cream." There was something about it that made him feel like a billion tiny bubbles were frothing up under him, keeping him buoyant in a silky, white sea.

He took Theatre Studies all through high school, not because he wanted to be an actor but because he needed the creative outlet. Even so, his teacher said he showed promise, and Dennis respected the man's opinion. That teacher was big on trust exercises with blindfolds. Dennis's favourite was the Tropical Sensory Getaway that ushered participants through a thrilling adventure of touch, hearing, taste, and smell.

First off, he was blindfolded and led onto "the cruise ship," which was really just a chair but by that point his disbelief had been fully suspended. The teacher honked a bicycle horn to signal his departure from port, and he was off. One of his peers ate Cheezies and blew in his face to simulate the bracing tang of an ocean breeze. Two of the taller guys rocked his chair back and forth to evoke the motion of the waves, and the prettiest girl in the class misted him gently with her hairspray. When he arrived at "the beach," which was really just a box of sand, he took off his shoes and socks and wiggled his bare toes with abandon. Then somebody handed him a pineapple juice box and he had never tasted anything so sweet and exotic in all of his life.

DENNIS EATS HIS BURGER, and it's delicious. He savours the spongy bun, the softly yielding tomato slice, the dill pickle with its knobby skin like that of an alligator. And of course the patty itself, pebbled and slightly chewy with the flavour of distant pastures and the kind of full blue sky that made his stomach hurt with possibility when he was a young man at the beginning of his life and used to go on car rides with his mom, and whenever they passed a farmer's field she would shout, "Dennis! Cows!"

And though the baklava and honey balls and rice pudding on offer may all be very tempting, for dessert tonight he will indulge in poetry.

BROWN HAIR. JEANS, A pair. Black boots. Voice hoots.

Truthfully, the poet doesn't sound like an owl, but Dennis is pleased with his spontaneous verse nonetheless. Maybe he'll share it with her later, when the performances have concluded, to show his appreciation for the poem she is sharing with him and a few other people now.

After paying his bill and liberally remunerating the fair

waitress for her service, he'd moved from his table to one of the chairs arranged around a small stage at the other end of the restaurant. When the waitress saw him sitting there a few minutes later, she rolled her eyes at the empty microphone and said, "Have fun." He replied, "I'm looking forward to it!" She laughed more, which gave him the same joyous, bubbly feeling that the word "cream" has always elicited.

The young female poet's offering is more of a non-rhyming love story. All the same, her words transport Dennis to a distant yet comfortably familiar locale. He can visualize the hay bales in the dilapidated barn she is describing, and the ravishing farmer's daughter lying back on them with her generous spill of corn-silk hair, which means blond in a more poetic way. The broad-shouldered farmhand lying beside her utters a manly grunt — which upon reflection is similar to the sound Dennis made when he finished his burger — indicating his satisfaction with either the farmer's daughter or the pleasantly scratchy cushion of hay. Dennis isn't sure at first, but that's what's called suspense.

Despite the drama unfurling from the microphone, however, he senses a restlessness from his fellow audience members. Some are sighing, others are shuffling in their chairs, and several are indiscreetly checking their mobile devices instead of enjoying the sheer entertainment right here in front of them.

Dennis is trying valiantly to pay attention to the engaging tale being spun from this woman's fetching red lips that are speaking these words that she herself wrote in an act of sheer invention. Literature! He is completely invested in the raw emotion being splattered onstage, even though apparently it's not quite up to snuff for the majority of this gloomy crowd.

He himself prefers to have fun and roll with life, and if he spontaneously wants to go out for a burger or even pizza, he'll do it. And if a nice-looking woman comes in and orders an extra-large with pepperoni, mushrooms, and double cheese while he's sitting down to enjoy his evening slice, he might say, "There's a free table over here, Miss." And she might give him a funny look and say, "I'm getting an extra-large pizza to go, but thank you." Then he says, "Hey, a big appetite is attractive on a woman." And she says, "It's for my family, at home," and waits by the cash register until her food is ready.

*Suit yourself*, Dennis beams out at the sighers and shufflers and device-checkers, who don't seem to realize how difficult it is to craft a tale from nothing and to create believable characters who people can empathize with.

THE TRICK IS, YOU need to pose the question, *How can I locate some common feeling with this individual who is outside my own realm of personal experience?* Because in art and everyday existence, we can all benefit from stepping into the shoes of others.

For example, as Dennis learned from that wise Theatre Studies teacher of yesteryear, you could envision yourself as another actual human being or a fictional fabrication of one, or even as someone in an advertisement, who is really just an actual human being pretending to be someone else. Such as the man in the poster he saw in the restroom of this very establishment.

It was an ad for gum, and the idea of the campaign was to have safe breath in the event that a person encountered romance. "Safe" in this case meaning minty fresh after chewing this particular brand of gum, apparently, so that you would make a positive impression when you started kissing a stranger. In the ad, the man was kissing a woman with porcelain skin and dark curly hair, and they were both smiling so as to convey their mutual enjoyment of each other's breath. And, one would assume, sexual arousal as well.

So Dennis put himself into this guy's shoes, even though technically he couldn't see them because the picture only showed the couple from the shoulders up. But regardless, there he was, locking lips with this heavenly brunette creature, and it was snowing and he was wearing a leather jacket, a fashionable choice but not very warm so he was shivering but trying not to show it because shivering is not a manly action. The woman was wearing a red toque with a giant pom-pom, which he thought was stupid — such an alluring lady wearing a dumb hat like that? But he decided not to say anything because he wanted to keep her happy, and negative comments aimed at a female's wardrobe choices are often frowned upon by said females, or so he has heard. No, no — he wanted to stay in her good graces and thereby encourage her to keep kissing him forever.

Okay, they could maybe pause to get married and have a couple of children together. And one day she would stop at a pizza place on her way home from work and order an extra-large pizza for him and the kids, and they'd all sit down at the table and dig in, and the kids would say, "Mmm, pizza!" Dennis and his wife would hold hands even when they were eating, and after they put their little boy and girl to bed they'd wink at each other, which was their code for "adult time." Meaning he was going to crawl all over her and do all sorts of things to her, and she was going to let him.

ONSTAGE, THE POET HAS her farmhand fumbling around in the pockets of his dusty jeans — oh no, what does he have in there? A knife? Should the farmer's daughter be afraid of her darling farmhand? How well do they really know each other anyway, after merely a few dalliances in the barn and the stables and the cold cellar?

Sure, they've just made extremely passionate love, with nobody to witness that passion save for an errant lamb who wandered in at a crucial point and made them chuckle at its frightened bleating that contrasted its soft, woolly innocence against the violent throes of their mutual orgasms. But when you get down to brass tacks, he is a mysterious farmhand without a past who was hired by her blind and therefore overly trusting father on a whim when he showed up one day bearing a mysterious scar that remained unseen by the farmer, due to the blindness.

He is also poor. In fact, the farmhand's Achilles heel — literary parlance for weakness — is his crippling insecurity about his finances. As well as his general lack of mental skills. Otherwise why can't he earn a decent living? Even though he can ride a horse with his eyes closed, and we're not talking about a gentle animal here. We're talking the craziest steed of the bunch, who bucks constantly and has a thirst for human blood, which is unusual for horses.

But the farmhand is certainly working very hard as a farmhand, there's no doubt about that, and in fact he caught the eye of the farmer's daughter in the first place when he was huffing and puffing from exertion while wrangling. He became so overheated that he had to take his shirt off, and the daughter couldn't help but notice all the sweat dripping down his hard muscles. She offered him a paper towel, which didn't do much absorbency-wise but he appreciated the gesture all the same.

ISN'T EVERYBODY LOOKING FOR a way to make more money these days? Dennis's plan is to create a revolutionary online game where users can scan a photo of their head, which they would float around and plunk onto different bodies, such as a runway model or Olympic athlete or Dracula. Even various animals would be available.

It will be like a virtual out-of-body experience, which Dennis had last month in real life when he slipped on some ice and fell backwards onto concrete. He lost consciousness and the next thing he knew, his soul was performing the very tricky manoeuvre of hovering above his prone, motionless form. He gazed at himself and felt there was something important he wanted to say, but then he travelled to a whole other galaxy where the peaceful, squid-like inhabitants of a planet much like ours, only colder, worshipped him as a god.

They explained that they had the power to grant wishes and asked was there anything he was truly in need of, deep down in his soul? And he said it would be appealing to partner up love-wise with a nice-looking lady. The aliens said, "Sure, why not?" And he was thinking, *All right, here we go!* Then boom, he was back on Earth again, lying on the sidewalk and staring up at the bright blue sky. A nice-looking woman passing by frowned down at him with concern, and he thought, *Thank you, aliens.* He was about to ask for her number but then he passed out again, and woke up alone in the hospital with a concussion. Which was where his online game idea was born.

His users will have the opportunity to step into the shoes of an Ancient Egyptian pharaoh or a cheetah, or perhaps a tough yet tender farmhand. And through the magic of social media they'll be able to communicate with each other, such that a user pretending to be a fireman could send a message to a user pretending to be a prima ballerina, like, "If you were dancing and your house was burning down, I would save you but only if you took all your clothes off and started touching yourself."

In an early brainstorming session, Dennis also conceived the character of the handsome but emotionally unavailable and frequently sarcastic cultural studies major he roomed with in university who was always banging different chicks. The scenario: You're him, and you're lying in bed reading some porn, and there is a timid knock at your door. It's the girl from down the hall who wears leather shorts all the time and makes collages with found materials, which basically means garbage. She giggles shyly and asks can she sleep beside you?

Just sleep and no sex or anything. And you say, "Sure, okay. But you better make sure there's no s-e-x, like you said." And that funny remark causes her to laugh and makes her want to have sex with you after all. In fact, she starts begging because she really, really wants it. So eventually you decide to be nice and give it to her.

There will be an element of danger as well, such as the threat of a horrific online death if players do not sufficiently immerse themselves in their chosen personas, which will have to be measured by some sort of empathy barometer.

All he needs now is a clever name for the website, and some game developers, and he's ready to go.

MEANWHILE, BACK AMONG THE hay bales, the author is using the skillful technique of poetic justice as the farmhand produces a diamond ring from a pocket of his tight, worn denims and asks for the farmer's daughter's hand in marriage. So clearly this will not be a tragedy after all, even though the farmhand could just as easily have pulled a cruel blade out of his pants instead. They embrace, and the farmer's daughter shouts an ecstatic "Yes, oh, yes!" The farmhand slides the ring onto the farmer's daughter's finger, and swears he will protect her forever.

"Safe," Dennis breathes. "You will always be safe with me."

And then he kisses the farmer's daughter, obviously, because what else is there to do once a proposal has been made and accepted? He closes his eyes and sinks into pure physical sensation. Her lips are soft and malleable like the creamiest of rice puddings, her breath has the intoxicating sweetness of pineapple, and her hairspray tickles his nostrils like the finest of sea mists.

At that moment, he hears a strange and menacing combination of sounds — low groans and snickers along with a restless tapping and shuffling only partially masked by a cacophony of coughs. The source of these noises is not immediately evident, so he tells the achingly beautiful farmer's daughter — his betrothed! — to stay where she is while he investigates.

With his lowered eyelids impairing his vision, he puts his remaining senses on high alert. His nostrils widen to sniff out the threat above the whimsical scents of straw, sawdust, and dung. His fingers scuttle stealthily around the pen he keeps tucked in his shirt pocket in case inspiration strikes — he could use it as a weapon if brute force doesn't suffice. He tastes beef on his tongue, which is distracting. Didn't he consume a romantic picnic lunch of fried chicken and cucumber sandwiches with his gal before their splendorous liaison in the barn?

"Be brave," he urges his trembling fiancée. He will hunt down the cruel beast hissing at her from the shadows and slay it with his large, calloused hands.

Then the two of them can go back to what they were doing before she agreed to be his wife. Haha, okay, sure, and then she can get started on the wedding plans. He smiles at her indulgently. He likes a woman who knows what she wants.

But hold on a minute here, because there's something weird about her head. Right before his eyes it's dissolving, whirring, flapping like birds. Then the colour bleeds out of the hay bales, the chairs, the stage, and the dish of thick, luscious cream for the barn cat, and he thinks, *No, not wings — leaves.* So many of them, and all from different trees. Even though it was winter the last time he checked. Where did all this crazy autumn foliage come from?

And just when he's beginning to suspect that things may not be exactly as they seem, his beloved reaches her long, reassuring arms towards him, and applauds. And mutters something that sounds like, "Thank fucking God."

Dennis wakes up. He blinks rapidly. He looks around. He sits straighter in his chair and claps more exuberantly than everyone else. He is suddenly alight with ideas. He is on fire. The perfect title for his online game pops into his brain, and he is full of love for the universe and immensely grateful for the inspiration it bestows upon him every day, like a shiny gift.

The host of the evening steps up to the microphone and slings his arm around the poet's thin shoulders. She slumps a little under the weight, but she's beaming.

He says to her, "That was great. You're great. I'd really like to talk to you more about that piece later, because it really moved me."

The poet nods and blushes until he lets her go. When she returns to her seat, several people lean in and whisper loudly to her, "That was so amazing!"

The host is wearing a tuxedo — *just like the man in the painting*. He is younger than Dennis, but much taller, and with a carefully trimmed handlebar moustache that gives him additional authority, plus coolness. "I see some new faces here tonight, which is awesome. We do this every Wednesday, guys, so put it on your calendars. Big thanks to the proprietors of Athena's Grill for providing this space for us to exorcise our creative demons. They also changed my diapers, which I guess is another thing I should thank them for. Except they also make me tell you to come early and order food first. Ideally one of the more expensive dishes, like the moussaka or the calamari dinner. Or the shrimp saganaki, which is my personal favourite. Or a burger, whatever. Just eat something to keep the old Greek people off my back, or else they're going to zap me with their evil eye."

*The host is the magical pear painter*, Dennis realizes with a gasp. *And he just mentioned burgers and I had a burger.*

"And please don't forget to tip our lovely waitress gener- ously, because she works like a dog." The host sticks his hands in his pockets — *just like the man in his painting!* — and grins at the waitress as she walks by, but she's very focused on balancing her tray of empty glasses. "Okay!" he says. "We've got a great crowd here tonight so if you've got something special to share with us, now's your chance."

Dennis can hardly believe his ears. *Anyone can do this?* And the click-clack of the waitress's heels is the sweet sound of serendipity.

"Remember, there's no time limit, and the sky's the limit. Anything goes. Just get up here and wow us."

Dennis's heart races with the thrill of a freshly minted fictional tale that his mind has crafted on the spot, with barely any effort at all. The best part is the ending, which concerns the newly clarified understanding of a previous "reality" that the protagonist has upon rousing himself from a deep slumber.

The host angles a palm over his eyes like he's shielding them from bright sun, and surveys the audience. "So, who's next?"

Dennis thinks, *I am*.

He raises his hand, and holds his breath, and waits.

# AT KIMBERLY'S PARTY

WE ALL KNEW SHE'D be the one. It wasn't like it wasn't obvious. She was right there in front of us all along, doing well. But the thing that makes us mad is that she doesn't deserve it.

She always whined about what she had. She'd get a good thing and we'd all tell her, "You're so lucky." And she'd say, "Yeah, I am lucky. Thanks, you guys." Then the next day she'd call one of us up and start whining again.

She'd say something like, if the good thing she had was a guy, "But I don't know if he really loves me." Or if the good thing was good marks, like she always got, she'd say, "But I don't know if I can keep this up until university. I have to keep this up until university." And we'd say, "He loves you," or, "Of course you'll keep it up."

The one time she actually got drunk enough to puke, we were all there for her. She didn't like to drink back then because she was scared of new experiences. But at Kimberly's party she finished a whole mickey of dark rum all by herself and then she puked in Kimberly's little brother's toy box, and we were all there, cleaning the chunks off Matthew's Pogs and Boglins. We said to everybody, "This is her first time."

And when she found a new friend, who lured her in with compliments about how smart and pretty she was — because we never gave her compliments about those parts of her, apparently — we sat back and let it happen because she'd never had that many friends, aside from us, so why shouldn't she branch out a bit?

But very quickly we could see that this new friend was no good for her. The new friend didn't care about her like we cared about her. So we told the new friend, in no uncertain terms, to get lost.

We liked it better anyway when it was just our little gang. And we could tell she preferred that too. Even when she wrote us that long letter in grade nine or ten saying our friendship was hurtful to her, it didn't make any sense and we didn't believe a single word. We tore it up and watched the pieces flutter to the ground, and we said to her, "Do you see that? That's you without us."

Because she needed to know how much we valued her, and everything she had to offer.

She was constantly making us laugh, for instance, with her weird stories that she made up off the top of her head. Although it's interesting that for someone with such a supposedly great sense of humour, she never got that we were only joking when we did the things we did.

Did she think we were being serious those times when

we'd all eat lunch outside the school on beautiful days, and we'd sprinkle handfuls of grass on her fry gravy? Because we'd always help her pick off the grass afterwards, and there was never any dirt like she said there was. Plus, in the process of throwing out the bad fries, she had to get rid of the ones that had the most gravy on them, which was ultimately good for her. Because she was a bit heavier in those days and she really didn't need to be eating so much unhealthy food, which we tried to explain to her, but in a lighthearted way so she wouldn't feel too self-conscious.

We appreciated her weird stories when nobody else did. We told her she was funny, when before the only other people who told her she was funny were her family.

We were her family too. She grew up with us. Her parents loved us, welcomed us into their home with open arms. When the new friend abandoned her, we went over and her mom let us in with a look on her face like, "She needs your help, girls." We went to her and we comforted her.

Then she went away to university and lost some weight and started dressing nicer and going to concerts, and we went to visit her and she was different. She had changed. She pretended like she was glad to see us, but she wasn't. It was a very painful time for us. She was growing out of our reach and meeting new people every day, and what's that saying, "Make new friends but keep the old. One is silver, the other gold." We were her gold, and she threw us away. Who throws away gold?

We called her mother and told her we were concerned. Her mother said, "She seems fine to me." We hung up on her mother.

We tried to forget about her after that, but we couldn't. Whenever we got together — without her, obviously — we said to each other, "Remember her? The way she wore clothes that her mother picked out for her all the time? That was hilarious." And, "Remember how she used to draw those pictures of our teacher, with fire coming out of his mouth? And how she used to draw those goofy cartoons of herself, with the frizzy hair, and she always drew the speech bubble next to her face that said, 'Get me out of here!!' That was a riot, wasn't it?"

And one of us might say, "We should give her a call." But we never did.

Then one day we saw her name in the paper, with an announcement, and we all went to the place where the announcement in the paper said she would be. We had to buy tickets ahead of time, which was annoying. But friends make sacrifices for each other, and we were sure that if she'd known we were coming she would've put us on the guest list, or at least offered us a discount.

There were a lot of other people in the audience, and they laughed a lot. Some of them even mouthed along with some of her routines, which they seemed to know by heart.

We didn't think much of her show, but we were full of anticipation about surprising her at the end of it. We thought, *A reunion!* It was going to be awesome. She was going to be so happy to see us, being there to support her like old times.

And she was happy, at first. Or, as we later learned, only on the surface. Our old teacher was there too, and he was so proud of her, and in front of him she smiled at us and clasped her hands and said, "Oh, it's so nice to have the little gang back together again!" Even though the teacher was never part of our gang, and he probably wouldn't be so proud anymore if we showed him those mean pictures she drew, which we kept because that's what friends do — they treasure their memories of each other.

We all made plans to go out for dinner, but without the teacher, and she even let us pick the place. She said, "I don't remember what's good here anymore." We picked the best place we could think of, and it seemed to go well.

But then afterwards we emailed her and said, "That was fun! We should do it again!" And she emailed us back and said she was sorry, but she had moved on with her life, and we were in the old part, which was the part she didn't want to think about anymore, and she was sorry but she didn't want to see us again, ever.

What were we supposed to do? We weren't going to beg. Did she expect us to beg? We had to forget her like she wanted to forget us. We had to forget about the good times, like the jokes and the fire coming out of the teacher's mouth, and the bad times like at Kimberly's party, except that wasn't even a bad time in the end, because we all came together, like sisters, and took care of her the best we could.

# PRIZE

THIS WOMAN I KNOW, who had a baby? She told me she has way more skin tags now. They're all over her body. And she isn't going to get them removed. She said she can't be bothered, which tells you something. She also said I can look forward to the fate of stubbing my toes daily on multi-coloured plastic shit that plays music that will make me want to kill myself. That was her exact phrasing, which I thought was pretty funny, but she said it wasn't funny at all.

The thing is, and Allen and I are in total agreement on this, it's all about having a positive and loving outlook. If you truly want the child you're bringing into the world, then your gratitude for that child is going to cancel out all the bad stuff. For example, if you trip and hurt yourself on a toy that was previously amusing your infant, you just say, "Oopsie!" You don't blame a little baby for a simple accident. Similarly, if you get a skin tag, you go to the dermatologist and get it zapped with a laser. You don't kick your kid in the face for making you less attractive. I'm not saying that's something that this woman who had the baby did. Although I wouldn't put it past her. She's not a close friend or anything.

THE WAY ALLEN AND I are going to pay for our baby is, we're building an Escape Room. Allen works in data administration and I'm currently a cashier but I have my diploma in business communications so we're already in an advantageous position, combined-projected-earnings-wise. However, I do agree with Allen that we need to get in on the ground floor of this emerging trend in extreme recreation while the getting is good. We're keeping our plan a secret for now because not a lot of people know what an Escape Room is, but once they do, everybody will jump all over it and try to cash in on our cow, which is also supposed to be our nest egg.

I certainly know the feeling of being bored with life, and it turns out that this is a very normal feeling because more and more average citizens are attempting to make their lives more exciting by engaging in risk-taking behaviour during their leisure time. Specifically, people are paying good money to get locked in a room with no obvious way out.

A few weeks ago, Allen's company sent him on a team-building exercise to one of our competitors. His team didn't win, but nonetheless it gave us a rock-solid strategy for improving our shared future, which was the main takeaway. Plus the experience taught him that he can't count on anybody, and that was a valuable lesson to learn.

The idea is, if you can't read the clues properly and instead of escaping you end up crouched alone in the corner from helplessness and terror, it means you're bad at cooperating with your fellow employees and when you get back to your office everybody will know it. I'm not saying this applies to Allen, but his manager, Devon, said that it did.

Fortunately, none of that impacts Allen because Devon is so useless at her job that she makes him sit with his back to the entrance of his cubicle. That is pretty much the worst possible seating arrangement a so-called "higher-up" could ever enforce on a so-called "underling," since it results in the person with his or her back to the open space being so twitchy they can't ever properly concentrate on their work, which is why Allen often doesn't produce to the level Devon says he should be producing to. Also she has a stupid stuck-up name like out of a soap opera, so who does she think she is?

It's like the other day when it was hot, but not hot enough for this woman who walked past me to be wearing a halter-top with short-shorts. She had a tiny dog with her and the dog was wearing a sweater, and I was thinking what an idiot to make her dog wear clothes when she was barely wearing anything at all. I personally was wearing capris and a T-shirt, which means I'm modest. That's one of the things Allen loves about me. He loves that I'm modest and he loves that I have a normal name like Amber instead of a stupid stuck-up bitch name like Devon.

Allen is my new boyfriend and he is pretty much the best thing that has ever happened to me.

Last night I dreamed that aliens had invaded, and one of the questions the alien invaders asked their human captives — me and my mom — was, "Do you have recurring ear infections?" And the people who said no — my mom — were sent into one room and the people who said yes — me — were sent into another.

My mom was looking really good due to the exercise classes she was taking, and before the aliens took her away she was telling me about her latest interaction with Sandy from Zumba, who made passive-aggressive comments all the time. Such as Sandy saying to my mother, "We feel it's a blessing that our grandson was born with a hole in his heart because having a grandchild with a birth defect is better than having no grandchild at all, right?"

My mom's head sagged at that point in the anecdote as it surely must have sagged after Sandy's barb during their original exchange, and then two praying-mantis-looking creatures grabbed her newly less-saggy arms and started dragging her off in the opposite direction from me.

Over in my pre-judgment pod I wanted to call out, "Sandy is an asshole, Mom, don't let her get to you. Plus, guess what? I'm pregnant!" But my voice was suddenly muted by an unseen force, and a sentry prepared to insert a probe into my ear and I knew I was in trouble because I'm an excreter — my doctor has told me on numerous occasions — meaning I produce too much wax and have to get it flushed out every few months. Of course I compound the problem because my ears get itchy so I scratch them and then they get crusty so I pick them. I know you're not supposed to use Q-tips but it is so deeply satisfying to dig around in there. My ex called it an ear-gasm and he laughed when I said I'd never heard that before, because apparently everybody in the world knows that super-common expression except for me, Dummy Dumb-Dumb over here.

So I just waved at my mom, even though I would've preferred to hug her because I could tell she was getting all worked up over the Sandy stuff again. Then the door for the people with recurrent ear infections slid open and foreboding music played from somewhere, something with oboes, and I thought, *That's a little melodramatic.* But these aliens were like that.

BASICALLY WHAT HAPPENED WITH me and my ex was we were going along quite comfortably in our lives together until one day he yanked the rug out from under us, and the rug was covered in dirt that I had not been aware of. But he — Ricky — said he knew the dirt had been there all along. So I was like, "Why didn't you clean it up, then?" And Ricky was like, "Well, it didn't bother me so I just left it there." And I was like, "So now it bothers you all of a sudden? I guess the vacuum cleaner weighs a million pounds and that's why you never pick it up." To which he said, "Babe, we are way too late for vacuum cleaners. Also I don't want to have kids with you, ever." To which I had no reply. I mean, what can you say to that? Except after he left I was thinking I could've said something like, "How about you just use the Swiffer? It's lighter and you don't have to rely on being near a power source." I'm not sure he would've understood the sarcasm, though.

When Allen moved into my apartment, he saw the possibilities immediately. I have one regular-sized closet that I use for my clothes, and one giant closet that I was using for basically nothing. Bits and pieces of my life with Ricky that I definitely should not have been holding on to. But I was, until Allen came along.

In a single afternoon he cleared out every piece of useless junk I'd been keeping in there, including Ricky's old tennis shoes and the vacuum cleaner with all of its negative connotations. Afterwards, I stood looking at the empty closet that was full of potential and I was like, "Oh my God, thank you, Allen. I can breathe now."

He said, "Attagirl," and gave me a gentle push as if to say, "The rest is up to you!" and he closed the door on me so I could fully appreciate the joy of being Ricky-free. It was pitch-black in there and I started getting a bit freaked out, but after several minutes he yanked the door back open and comforted me with sex because he knew exactly what I needed right then, which was closeness — and a baby.

I READ IN A magazine the other day that if you sign up online and pledge to perform one act from a list of pre-selected acts of kindness, you could win a prize. I thought, *What a fantastic way to get people to be nice to each other.*

The magazine was at my doctor's office where I was waiting for my first prenatal check-up and probably my bazillionth earwax flushing, and if Allen had been there with me — like he wanted to because that's the kind of boyfriend he is, but like he couldn't be because his manager is a control-freak whore — I would've grabbed his hand and squeezed it after becoming excited about the prospect of offering incentives to participants in our own venture. As in, along with the satisfaction of finding your way out, you also get a badge or certificate or Diploma of Escape, or something along those lines. Maybe a pen? It would have to be engraved, though. Allen has put me in charge of marketing because it's what I went to school for, so clearly I'm the right choice.

Allen is in charge of the heavy lifting, haha, but for real that's what he's doing because he's constructing the Escape Room's interior and exterior. He says he's making it foolproof and airtight and I said, "That's great, honey, but we don't want our clients to suffocate!"

Anyway, I haven't felt stimulated by my cashier job for a while so I'm loving the challenge of this new responsibility. I've been studying other companies' advertisements for inspiration, and there's one campaign I've seen everywhere lately that has made a big impression on me. It's for a bank, to show how easy banking can be and how fulfilling it is to take control of your finances by handing over that control to a financial planner. The people in the ads are skeletons.

I'm not sure what this aesthetic decision is supposed to communicate — maybe that even the dead need to be vigilant about their economic well-being? Halloween is a few months away, so it's not seasonal. The skeletons are quite frightening, as well. Some of them have bits of rotting flesh hanging off their bones. But in a decorative way, like the pieces of skin might be a necklace or a bracelet on the ladies or a tie or cuf-flinks on the guys. They seem happy enough, as skeletons go, laughing and joking with each other. On one poster I saw on the subway, the skeleton financial advisor is sitting across his desk from a skeleton couple and their skeleton baby. They are clearly excited to be planning their child's future. She has a long life ahead of her and they want to make that life as comfort-able and stress-free as possible, at least monetarily.

I don't think Allen and I are going to use skeletons in our Escape Room ads, and I already bank somewhere else so we probably won't go to this institution to start an RESP for our baby as a result of this particular campaign. Nonetheless, it's an attention-getter.

HERE IS SOMETHING I could picture my mother doing if she was a grandmother: She would babysit for us constantly. And when Allen and I would come home after reaffirming our coupledom by watching a movie or playing mini-golf or shop-ping for candles at HomeSense together, she would be eagerly waiting to report something new that our now peacefully sleeping baby had learned or accomplished.

I could picture her saying, with her grandmotherly eyes full of pride, "She noticed the breeze tonight! She felt it on her face. She closed her eyes, is how I could tell. And she lifted her chin just a tiny bit as the wind ruffled her hair. It wasn't much wind at all, but she definitely noticed it."

"That's wonderful, Mom," we would say.

Then Allen would kiss both of us and go to bed while my

mom and I would stay up and have Kahlúa Mudslides. We'd look through old photo albums from when I was a baby, and I'd tell her how grateful we were for her help, especially since so many new parents didn't have that kind of support, and as a direct consequence ended up in very unhappy family situations.

SOMETIMES MY HANDS GET dry, so I use lotion to moisturize them. It makes them slippery. Usually I'm in the bathroom when I do this because that's where I keep the lotion, and when I go to open the bathroom door, the knob won't turn due to the greasiness of my skin, so for a few seconds I'm totally helpless and trapped. Of course I'm not really trapped, but still. The possibility is there, you know?

I told Allen this is something we should consider exploring in our promotional material, like, "You can push and pull and knock and bang all you want, but you're never getting out of here! Mwahaha!" And he said, "Amber, you can be really funny sometimes." Which is a huge compliment coming from him. Even though I was mostly being serious. Allen is hilarious because when he answers his phone and sees it's me he says, "Pizza Pizza, how can I help you?" Or maybe he does that with everybody, I don't really know.

What I do know is, sex with Allen is tons better than it was with Ricky. With Ricky I had to fake it all the time, and with Allen I only have to fake it sometimes.

I guess the main problem with faking it is you don't let the other person see the true you, since you're robbing them of witnessing you when you're at your most vulnerable. I know

Allen never has an issue with me seeing him when his face goes all weird and rubbery and he's so caught up in the intensity of his own sensations it's like I'm not even there. Whereas I'm just all curled up inside sometimes, and it's not fair to him that I do that, I guess.

THE THING ABOUT ALLEN is that when I was a little girl I was chubby, and I only ever wore one-piece bathing suits. But when I was about twelve, I bought a pink-and-white leopard-print bikini at Giant Tiger and I'd put it on sometimes when I took a bath.

I had a fantasy where I would pretend I was swimming in a pond, and then I would gracefully emerge from the tub and gaze at my body in the mirror as if gazing at my reflection in the pond's still surface. Then a handsome teenage boy would swim over because he'd seen me from far away and thought I was so pretty he couldn't believe it. When he saw me up close I was even prettier, and he was too intimidated to talk to me at first but then he asked me out on a date and I said, "I don't know if I should." He said he wanted to kiss me and I said, "I don't even know your name." But I kissed him anyway.

When I met Allen at the bar after I broke up with my ex, he was drinking a beer and I was drinking a cooler, and he came over and said I looked nice and did I want another cooler because he was going to get himself another beer. It was just easy, and natural, and I realized he was like a grown-up version of the teenage boy in my fantasy, but in a real-life, non-pond type of way.

SO ALL OF A sudden Devon was in our Escape Room, and I wasn't really sure how I felt about that. Not very good, was the first feeling that sprang to mind.

One minute I was preparing my signature twist on macaroni salad, which has cut-up bits of bologna in it and is known in German parlance as *fleischsalat*, and the next minute Allen and I were having dinner with his boss, who I never in a million years expected to be having dinner with, but before she came over Allen said, "Just trust me on this." So I did.

He told me he'd devised this scheme to invite Devon over and we'd be all nice to her and then boom, he'd reveal our amazing Escape Room, and that would basically be him saying, "Amber and I are entrepreneurs now and we're going to be rich so I don't need a paycheque from you anymore thank you very much, plus you're a shitty manager. So fuck you, I quit!"

That sounded awesome to me, so I made the *fleischsalat* and put out some chips and dip — *Lipton onion soup mix, you've saved me again*, I thought — and microwaved some frozen peas because it wasn't like I had time to plan a meal and shop for it. I mean, what do you expect when you give me, like, zero notice that we're going to be entertaining a guest?

And then the three of us were sitting around the table, and I was on the alert for Devon's trademark bitchiness but she must've been on her best behaviour because we actually had quite a pleasant conversation. Although Allen mostly just sat there and ate his food because he's a man, and men generally don't have much to say when they're surrounded by women.

At one point he disappeared and then came back with drinks for us, which was sweet.

Devon and I talked about what having kids was like even though I don't really know what it's like yet. She had a bunch of goofy stories, mainly about how giving birth had ruined her body forever. For instance all the skin tags everywhere. I wanted to tell her something negative about my body too so I explained my disgusting earwax situation. Then I paused to reflect on how my boyfriend truly did love me for who I was, despite my imperfections.

Devon put a hand on my arm and said, "You know, Amber, it's so refreshing to meet you because you're a real person. All day I'm in meetings and it's 'mission critical this' and 'core competency that.' But here you are with your meat salad and your Bacardi Breezers and goddammit you are fucking real."

I couldn't help thinking, *Surely she must know there's a* purpose *to the language of business*, but she was being so nice that I kept that to myself.

She went on. "I have to tell you, when Allen said he wanted to meet outside of office hours to discuss a personal issue, I thought to myself, *No way am I going to this psycho's house!* I mean, the guy's always so quiet, right? You know what he's like. But then he said, 'I'd like you to meet my pregnant girlfriend Amber,' and I said, 'You have a girlfriend?' And here you are, and you're so normal." She took a deep breath and blinked a few times. "Woo, I'm feeling a little drunk! What per cent are they making these coolers nowadays?"

The next thing I knew, Allen said he had something to show

her, and maybe I could get dessert ready while they were gone. And I thought, *What dessert?* Okay, it's possible there was half a Deep 'n Delicious hiding somewhere at the back of the freezer, but give me a break.

ONE TIME I FOUND a boy who was lost. It was back when I was with Ricky, and I was out for a walk because he'd done something stupid as per usual. I can't remember what exactly, but it was something along the lines of him flirting with my friend Tiffany right in front of me, and I was like, "Rent a hotel, asshole." And Ricky was like, "That's not even how it goes, Amber." And I was like, "Oh, you always think you're so smart." And he was like, "Babe, I touched her boob by accident when I was reaching for my drink. You know how big Tiffany's boobs are!" So I did the shot of Jäger he'd bought me because fuck you, I'm having the Jäger, and I took off.

The boy was maybe six or seven years old, and he was sitting on a curb a few blocks from the bar wearing just a pair of jogging pants, which I thought was weird because it was cold outside. I remember that detail because when I called 911 to report a lost kid, the lady asked me to describe what he looked like and I said, "He's only wearing jogging pants." I wanted to be specific.

But it started off with me seeing him there all alone, and I said, "Where's your Mommy?" He didn't answer so I thought maybe he didn't speak English, which you'd think would be a problem, but luckily I know French from grade school and I'd learned some German phrases when Ricky and I went to the Canadian Oktoberfest. I said, *"Parlez-vous français?"* and *"Sprechen sie Deutsch?"* Then he stood up and ran.

It was late and who knows how many creeps were out on the street so I started running after him, and I called my mom because I have never been good in crisis situations, and she told me to call 911.

So then I'm on the phone with this lady, who truth be told was acting kind of snobby towards me because I was all hysterical and out of breath and she had like zero emotion in her voice. She asked for my location and I said, "I can't read the street signs because I'm going too fast!" To which Robot Bitch-face replied, "I need you to tell me where you are." I said, "All right, fine," and I slowed down, and then the boy was gone.

So we all know whose fault it is if anything happened to him.

DEVON GOES UPSTAIRS WITH Allen to see our Escape Room and there's me cleaning up the dirty dishes. Then it hit me like a hammer: *She didn't even know I existed until today.* Allen doesn't talk about me with his co-workers. I talk about him at work all the time. The girls are probably sick to death of hearing his name! And now he was showing this woman he supposedly hated this special thing that meant so much to both of us, without me. I started to feel like maybe Allen didn't deserve to hear about this great idea I had, which was to rent a party boat for our repeat clientele.

Of course we'd have to wait a few years until we turned a decent profit, but then it would be a business expense! The sunlight would be sparkling on the water like majestic jewels, and crazy-good music would be playing super loud, and people on shore would see us cruising by and they'd be really jealous and would wish they were on a party boat too, because everybody feels that way when they see a party boat.

Picture it: It's a gorgeous day and you're wearing sunglasses and feeling the breeze on your face and you've got a cocktail going, and you don't have anything else to do and you don't have anything to worry about. And you're having these killer conversations with everybody because you're all wasted and you're all on the same team. We're talking customer loyalty for life.

Imagining the sun and the waves and what shoes I'd be wearing calmed me down a bit, and it occurred to me that keeping this great idea to myself was just me being petty and that wasn't going to help anyone, so I'd probably still tell Allen about it anyway.

Then he came downstairs alone, and I was like, "Where's Devon?"

"She got all excited," he said. "She wanted to give it a whirl."

I said, "What? I thought you were just going to show her! It's not ready for a test run. We haven't written the clues yet, or decided on the prize or anything."

Then he shrugged — he shrugged! — so I put my hands on my hips and stood up straight and said, "Do you even want to go into business with me, Allen?"

To which he replied — get this — "How's that dessert coming along?"

I shook my head and told him, "I found some cake." I handed

him his piece and I didn't bother warning him that it might be stale.

THE LAST TIME I visited her in the hospital, my mom said the main regret she had about raising me was that she wasn't fully present for enough of my milestones because she was too busy trying to capture them on film. Of course now we have digital cameras, but my point is — and if my mom was still around she would totally not take offence to this because I'm pretty sure she knew how much I appreciated all the stuff she did for me — I am not going to make the same mistake with my own kid.

When you take a picture, you're so focused on how you want it to turn out that you miss what's right in front of you. I've got photos of me and Allen smiling with this or that scenery behind us, but do I remember how it felt to be with him on those supposedly special occasions? Nope. I was too busy posing and trying to get the right angle with my phone so my arm wouldn't be in the shot. It was the same with the selfie of me and my mom from that day — I was so fixated on keeping all the tubes and the I.V. and whatnot out of the frame that I didn't even properly enjoy her company.

So when my daughter, or son, is about to blow out the single candle on the first slice of birthday cake for her, or his, very first birthday, I will sit still and watch that candle get blown out. I'll clap and cheer and make a big fuss and maybe lick some icing off of those tiny fingers, because that's how much I'm going to love this baby — I won't even worry about germs or anything.

And, bottom line, Allen is either going to step up to the plate or he isn't. I'm hopeful, because he already has that reassuring, fatherly way about him. When all the banging and the yelling quieted down about an hour ago, I said, "Do you think we should check on her?" And he said, "Relax, she's fine." So I relaxed.

At the end of the day, regardless of what the future holds, I will be right there with this child for every important moment and every unimportant moment too. I'm going to look in those innocent, twinkly eyes every morning and say, "Mama's not going anywhere." Which means my kid will never be alone, and I will never have to wish for the rest of my life that I had paid attention.

# PUPPYBIRD

THE CHILD IS PERFECT and everybody says so. The mother has absolutely nothing to complain about. Everybody says that too.

"This kid!" they exclaim. "She's like a doll. How do you get through your day without eating her?" People talk a lot about eating her daughter. A cashier leans over the mother's frozen dinners and smiles at the baby in her stroller: "Ooh, look at you, I just want to gobble you up." A pharmacist shoves aside the mother's hydrocortisone cream and bares his teeth at the girl's chubby legs: "I will bite you all over!"

When the mother gets home she presses buttons on the microwave and examines her arm rash that is sort of shaped like a soaring dove and listens to a voicemail from her own mother, who is wondering why has it been so long since she's seen her yummy granddaughter? Why is she being kept away from that teeny-weeny tasty monkey? She baked a pie. Does the baby eat pie yet? She's bringing it over tomorrow. It's delicious like her granddaughter. But not nearly as sweet!

The mother does not want to eat her baby, or harm her in any way.

DURING THE PERIOD WHEN the father found out he was going to be a father, a lot of famous musicians were dying. Killing themselves, being killed by other people, being killed by objects.

For a while, the highlight of the father's day was scrolling through the obituaries in the entertainment blogs and making bets with his co-workers on who would show up there next, and the losers would have to buy the winners chicken fingers at the pub across the street with the statue of the terrier wearing shorts and a top hat, which always made the father laugh.

The father and many of his co-workers had all wanted to be in a band at earlier points in their lives. Not in a band together, because they hadn't known each other at the time. They had all wanted to play different instruments, and some of them had wanted to be the singers.

The father had the most musical knowledge so he ended up eating the most chicken fingers. But after a while it got to the point where he had to work really hard to find the names of the latest dead artists, even if they died in exciting ways, like for instance the red-haired oboe player from YouTube who posted that video of himself swallowing an egg — a whole egg! — and then privately choked to death on rice pudding a few days later, because everyone was so sick of hearing about all those dead musicians all the time and the media wasn't making such a big deal about reporting them anymore.

That took most of the fun out of it, and then one day the mother handed the father an envelope, and inside the envelope was a set of plastic keys that rattled.

WHEN THE BABY WAS a newborn, she slept so peacefully in her bassinette that passersby would grab the mother's arm and shake it. "Look at that," they would say. "Look at your adorable baby who is sleeping! So innocent, so unschooled about the world. Because she has not yet had the experience of attending school, that's probably why. How lucky, to not have to go to school yet or have any grown-up concerns. What a lucky, attractive baby. Look at her slumbering so nicely while the big, bad world unfolds around her."

It's true that the baby is beautiful with an agreeable personality. It makes things easier. The mother has heard stories about children who do not behave.

One of her Facebook friends is constantly posting about how annoying her kids are. She posts pictures of them playing in a sandbox or running through a field and writes captions such as, "Look at these stupid idiots!" Apparently the tipping point was when they kept whining about being bored and she told them to go and build a fence with their new electronic fence-building toy, which didn't build actual fences that you could touch but just computer-generated pictures of fences. Her kids replied in their whiny voices that they wanted something real, like a real-life experience such as a spooky haunted hayride with werewolves and scarecrows and pumpkins and maybe even a corn maze to get lost in and then she could find them and hug them in a reassuring way. And meanwhile Hallo-ween had been over for weeks.

AFTER THE MOTHER GAVE birth, the father's co-workers got together and purchased a card that they filled with congratu-latory phrases such as, "Way to go!" and "Welcome to the ride of your life, buddy!" and "Holy shit, babies are the best!" On the front was a black-and-white photograph of a newborn's wrinkly fist rising into the air. Floating next to it was a single rose, which was probably red but it wasn't possible to know for sure.

The father took a few weeks off to give the mother a break. He brought the baby to the park and sat on a bench and looked at her lying in her bassinette. Sometimes she moved slightly. He dangled toys in front of her but she didn't seem interested.

The mother was sleeping a lot and the father was lonely, so he took the baby to his office to introduce her to the gang.

John in Accounts Receivable made goofy faces at her and told the father she reminded him of his daughter at her age. "They grow up so fast! You're going to hear that from every-body but it's true. Kelly is eight now! It's nuts." John was helping Kelly make a beach-scene diorama for her geography class because they were studying the coup in Thailand. He was collecting those little paper parasols that come with fancy cocktails, which meant he had to drink a lot of them, har har. Instead of smoking on his break times, he was slowly cutting one regular-sized beach towel into numerous miniature beach towels. "You have to be devoted," he told the father. "You have to be all in with them, because they have tiny immature nerves that are developing at an insanely rapid pace, and those nerves can sense if the parents are not fully committed to being the best parents they can be."

John said becoming a father had made him very creative and also very greedy. All he wanted was a little time alone, for God's sake. "'Just get the hell away from me,' I keep telling her. She's always in my face. And the biggest problem is that she wants to watch different shows than I want to watch. I'm like, 'When am I ever going to be able to watch my own shows, Kelly?' And then it's another episode of her crime-solving poodle or whatever. That's what happens. That's what they do to you."

Janine in Human Resources reached over to caress the infant's soft skin and told the father, "I'm afraid of what my son is going to do to me when he's older. He's only three, but he's so strong already."

The baby sucked hard on the father's thumb. The father said, "Oh, I'm sure you don't have to worry about that. Do you?"

"Kids can hurt you." Janine had a purple mouse pad that was shaped like a pterodactyl. "They'll hurt you and hurt you and hurt you."

THE MOTHER HAS A bad dream.

She goes to the crib in the morning, and the baby looks different. Her eyelids are swollen and her tongue lolls out of her mouth. When the mother picks her up, the baby spits in her face.

The mother tries to take a quiet moment for herself but the baby has lost the ability to play contentedly on her own. She flails her arms and screeches as soon as the mother puts her down.

The days go on and the baby gets worse. She will not nap and she will not fall asleep at bedtime. She bites the mother and other children. She makes herself vomit after every meal and snack. She reaches into her diaper and smears her shit all over her crib and stroller. She masturbates in public places. Her curls fall out and her teeth sharpen into fangs. She grows a tail and foams at the mouth. She sprouts leathery wings out of her small, sloped shoulders. She cries and cries and is no fun to be with at all.

The mother takes the baby to the doctor and learns that these are all symptoms of a terrible, mysterious disease that will make the baby completely dependent for the rest of her life. She goes home and tells the father about the diagnosis and he explains that he no longer finds the mother attractive. She has gained too much weight and cannot fit into any of her regular outfits anymore. The father leaves, and the mother is alone with the child forever.

WHEN THE MOTHER'S BELLY was big and round, the father took her to the theatre to see a violent movie. She leaned her head on his shoulder and they ate popcorn in the dark and it all felt very romantic until a man was being whipped with chains by a group of other men and the mother whispered, "Maybe I shouldn't be watching this in case the anger penetrates my womb." Then she doubled over with a grunt.

The father wondered if maybe she was having a sort of hyper-empathetic attack on the roughed-up hero's behalf, because ever since she'd found out she was pregnant she had been feeling extra guilty about hanging up on telemarketers. Somebody selling something they didn't need would call during dinnertime and mispronounce one of their names, and the mother would sit and have a conversation with them for twenty minutes before politely explaining she wasn't interested but they had done a very good job of trying to convince her, and she wished them nothing but the best in life and good luck meeting their quota, she was sure they were going to do great. When she came back to her half-finished meal at the table, the father would ask, "Why?" And the mother would answer, "Because they're human beings, honey."

In the theatre, the screen filled with blood and the mother gripped the father's hand. "Puppybird just kicked me in there."

TOWARDS THE END OF the mother's first trimester, the father came home from work and said how about they call the fetus "Puppybird."

She thought that was cute and asked how he came up with it, and he said it was from a memory of a valentine he received as a small boy that had a cartoon of a flying dog with a bow and arrow that had been mildly frightening at the time, but in hindsight made him really happy. He winked. "Plus it's way too young to be called Dogbird."

"Oh." The mother pulled at her waistband, which had gotten tight. All of her clothes were getting tight. "Isn't that funny."

"It's just a nickname." He smiled at her. "Just while the baby's inside. When it's outside we'll think of something different."

The mother and the father didn't celebrate Valentine's Day

because it was too commercialized. The father said why should they put their love on display just because Hallmark told them to?

The mother said, "Who gave you the card?" She used a silly singsong voice to show she wasn't actually worried.

He shrugged. "Nobody special."

"Well, then." The mother kissed him. "Puppybird it is."

THE FATHER BUYS A colouring book for the baby without really looking at it first. He brings it home and sets it in front of the girl in her high chair with some crayons.

On the first page is a line drawing of a dolphin wearing a firefighter's hat. The father thinks, *Why?* On the next page is a cartoon pair of overalls that has no wearer, yet is still standing upright. Then a tiger balancing on an enormous donut. He thinks, *What kind of book is this?*

His daughter rubs colour across the tiger's grinning face, his big, sharp teeth.

The father flips ahead to an anthropomorphized mug of coffee. *Do children drink coffee? Do coffee mugs have arms and legs? I don't think so.* On the page opposite is a giant feather floating inexplicably over a dog with hearts for eyes.

The baby shrieks and throws the crayons on the floor.

"You're right," says the father. "Let's put this away."

They go to the playground instead. Now that his daughter can crawl around and amuse herself, the father enjoys taking her there sometimes.

While he is waiting for her at the bottom of the slide, two older kids arrive.

"Hey," says the girl, "look at that stupid baby over there!"

"Yeah," says the boy, "babies are the stupidest!"

The boy is shirtless and the girl is wearing what appears to be a studded collar around her neck. They are maybe in grade two.

When the father was their age, he received a valentine from a classmate named Agatha who had freckles on her cheeks. He wanted to take a pen and connect all of those beautiful straw-berry-coloured dots to make a rocket ship or a submarine. He wanted to chase her and catch her and push her down.

The kids take running leaps onto the swings and flap their thin arms instead of holding on.

The boy shouts, "I bet she poops her pants all day long."

"Haha!" screams the girl. "She can't even go down the slide by herself. She still needs her daaaaddy."

The father expects the baby to cry, but she seems oblivious to the abuse. She squeals and laughs and wants to ride the bouncy squirrel.

He is in awe of her resilience.


THE MOTHER IS ALONE with the baby in the bathroom. The baby is having a bath and the mother is drying her hair.

The baby points her soft arm at the mother as she brushes and flicks and musses.

"Mama is getting ready," she says, and her daughter babbles over the sounds of her own splashing and the whoosh of the blow-dryer.

The baby has a favourite storybook that is full of words like *plop* and *zap* and *sizzle*. The plotline revolves around an orphaned gosling who is raised by a comically hungry ferret, but the best part is the noises. The mother's parents like to brag that when the mother was a baby, her first word was "onomatopoeia," although she has never really believed them.

The mother switches off the blow-dryer and buries it in the bottom of a drawer. She puts the baby to bed and tells the sitter there is food in the fridge if she wants.

Soon after, she and the father are sitting in a restaurant.

The father says, "Why does bread from a basket taste so much better than bread from a bag?"

The mother says, "I think the baby would like this place."

He looks around and nods.

"Okay," she says. "Now we should have a conversation about something besides our child. Shouldn't we?"

He reaches across the table and touches her hand. "Do you remember when all those musicians were dying?"

The mother blinks around at the other diners as if she is under a very bright light. "I can't remember my own name sometimes."

Afterwards, they walk along a street with lots of art galleries. It's getting late but the mother isn't ready to go home yet, so they wander into a room showing photos of people being tortured in various poses.

The gallery owner introduces herself and reassures them that none of the subjects were tortured in real life — the artist is actually making a statement against torture.

The father reaches for the mother again but she shakes her head. "They really look like they're in horrible pain."

The gallery owner smiles. "That's the beauty of it."

THE MOTHER AND FATHER remember a time before they had the baby, before they were married, before they were even living together, and friends of theirs asked them to housesit while they spent a week at a resort in Jamaica.

Once they had the place to themselves, the mother wandered through the many rooms and thought about how she would have decorated each one differently. One of them was the Baby's Room, with giraffe wallpaper and a rug that looked like a teddy bear that had been hunted and killed. Their friends did not have a baby yet but they were actively planning for one. They said they would be pregnant by the fall, and they were. But right then it was the spring and it was nice to pretend that the house belonged to her and the father and that they were married like their friends were.

The father had bought a bunch of his favourite foods, bacon and eggs and croissants, and he hummed as he put everything away. There was also a huge, ripe honeydew melon that they sliced open, and the juice got all over their fingers and they didn't even care.

The fridge had an ice machine, and the father made them gin-and-tonics with two cubes in each glass. The mother said, "I'd like three cubes, please," and the father said, "You always want more than I can give you." The mother said, "What is that supposed to mean, isn't there unlimited ice in there?" And he said, "I was joking, it was a joke."

Later on they smoked a tiny joint that the father said he'd been saving for a special occasion, and the mother got tired. She rested her head on the father's lap and closed her eyes.

The father wanted to go for a walk and the mother said, "All right, fine," but afterwards they were going to come back and lie down and eat ice cream.

They meandered through the unfamiliar subdivision with its identical crescents and courts and houses that were imitations of each other and neighbours who never used their front yards. Why would you have a front yard and not use it?

They held hands and felt superior and ran down the street. They jumped over small, multi-coloured bags full of dog poop and passed men watching TV in their garages and women watching TV in their family rooms, and they laughed because how funny and how pathetic. They kept running and yelled, "We will never live in a place like this!" even though the mother thought it would be a nice type of place to raise a family. An ice cream truck drove by and she pointed at it, but the father said, "Let's just enjoy the moment. Can't we just enjoy the moment?"

They were going so fast they nearly tripped over an abandoned tricycle. It was pink and had streamers and a horn with a fat, smiling duck head that quacked when you squeezed it, and they laughed even louder and both of them thought, *Isn't that absolutely perfect?*

Eventually, they came to an empty playground. They swung on the swing set like little kids. They scaled the monkey bars, and the father pounded on his chest like a gorilla and made the mother laugh. They decided not to play in the sandbox because neither of them wanted to get dirty, and anyway they didn't have shovels or buckets. Then the mother climbed to the top of the slide, and the father waited for her at the bottom.

# FLAMINGO

THE TWO OF US had booked some time off to visit a small town that was internationally known for its gummy candies. Every single one was apparently lovingly handcrafted by a little old woman in a little old house that was now a major tourist attraction with its own sign on the highway. The woman didn't do the advertising herself. She had a team. All she did was make gummy goats or pizza slices or lightbulbs or teeth. Basically whatever she felt like making. We were going to purchase a couple of her so-called "one-of-a-kind" confections and then, as a way of denying their specialness, eat them really quickly.

Around the back of the house there was supposed to be a rosebush with blooms that resembled children's faces. That was another reason for our impending trip, although not the main reason. We had read about this place in the travel section of the newspaper. The writer gave it a rave review. He said the flowers were a stunning example of nature at its freakiest. He said the gummy xylophone he had consumed had endowed him with superhuman strength. He said bring your kids if you have them, or just go alone. It was a wonderful experience for the young and the young-at-heart alike.

We thought, *Good*.

We had been parents once. After that didn't work out, we went to Las Vegas. Everyone was sad there, which was a disappointment because we were expecting to have fun. There were these flamingos, just standing on a little circle of fake grass next to a fake, I don't know, I guess it was supposed to be a lagoon. We were drunk when we saw them. We wanted them to perform for us, but they didn't. They were pretty quiet. Do flamingos even make sounds? They were pink, and their legs were like sticks. That was pretty neat. But it's not like that was them doing anything exceptional. It's just the way flamingos are.

We had a good amount of sex in our hotel room. I got all into a frenzy the first night and crawled across the carpet on my hands and knees and Greg was like, "Yes!" Then we hit the casinos and did some gambling, and drank too much butterscotch schnapps at a dance club that had a female midget in a fairy costume hooked up to a wire on the ceiling. The next day we hit the mall and did some shopping, and we hit the Whole Foods to grab an assortment of microbrews with amusingly offensive names like "Bang That Bitter Bitch!" and ate at the buffet there because it's organic. Then we went back to the casinos and gambled some more. We went to Fremont Street and paid five dollars to have our picture taken with two fat girls dressed up in American-flag bikinis and feather boas, even though their lack of enthusiasm made us feel vaguely uncomfortable.

We passed a blind guy begging for change and Greg said to me, "I'm glad I'm not blind. Have you seen blind people?" Which is his joke that he always tells so I've heard it a million times already, but I still laughed.

Not every couple is like that, with the easy sort of jocularity we enjoy. Take for instance my friend Jeanie, who is pregnant and therefore will probably never get to Las Vegas. She and her husband Stuart do not have very good chemistry. They listen to different types of music and watch different types of movies. And yet Jeanie told me she is looking forward to embarking on the adventure of parenthood with this man she doesn't even seem to like very much. She said that along with their cherished friends, like us  because Greg and I have all this free time now, is I guess her line of reasoning — they will team up to protect this tiny, vulnerable new person from all the evils in the world.

I said, Good luck. Because that's impossible.

I told her I had read a news story about a man who had murdered another man with a crossbow at a library. A witness said, "He just walked in and walked out, but not in a hurry or anything." Back between the shelves, there was a hole in the chest of a man who had been browsing the self-help section. He had been reaching for a book about how to turn grey skies sunny when the arrow pierced his heart, but of course he didn't know it was an arrow at the time — or later, even. He probably felt a sort of thunking sensation, then a lot of pain. In that moment, he might have been making plans to pick up falafels for lunch with his wife, and reflecting how she never got onions on hers because she said the taste of them would stay with her all day. He was maybe thinking of saying to her, *I'd like to stay with you all day*, and hoping she would laugh and slap his arm and say he was silly. But instead she would scowl and roll her eyes and say she needed some space — Jesus, could she just get some space once in a while? Later on, his killer was interviewed and he said he had become enraged earlier that day when he walked past a kids' birthday party in the park and realized he would never be as carefree and full of joy as those children had appeared to be.

That night I'd gone online and clicked on the mobile Jeanie and Stuart had registered for. We had never used a mobile because nobody had ever bought one for us. Theirs had a jungle motif. I pictured this helpless newborn staring up at those dangling monkeys and tigers and elephants going around and around. If that was me, I'd be like, *Holy shit, what are those things? Are they going to drop down here and eat me?* So I changed my order to some receiving blankets and a Moses basket, even though I don't exactly believe in God anymore.

I used to believe in God. I used to wake up every morning and switch on my coffee maker and get our son out of his crib and read him stories and kiss his face until he squealed and then I'd marvel at the fact that this perfect human being had actually picked us out of all the possible parent combinations he could have chosen, and then we'd have breakfast.

But I can see now that when you have such a rigid and fixed routine, that's what makes time speed up. When you're doing the same repetitive things over and over, that's when your life goes on fast-forward and eventually you open your eyes one day and think, *Where did all that time go?* I mean, holy crap, that's a lot of time that went by.

So what you need to do is you need to mix things up. Do something different once in a while. Like journeying halfway across the province to get some wiggly bonbons and look at some weird roses.

In the days leading up to our excursion, *bam!* suddenly time started slowing down for me. I was noticing details that had entirely escaped my attention previously. My coffee still tasted like coffee, yes, but I could also detect a smokiness or an earthiness in this or that particular brew. And I was savouring it! I was gazing out my window and seeing a lady walking her dog in the park across the street. The dog was wearing a sweater, and that made me laugh. I was recognizing the comedy in those types of small, everyday moments. Dogs don't need to wear sweaters because they already have coats, right? Of course.

Then it was time to leave, so we packed up our family sedan that was too large for the two of us, but came in handy for our suitcases. As we drove, Greg told me there's a secret lab in Haiti where scientists are turning innocent people into zombies via ancient voodoo methods and using modern pharmaceuticals. The zombies just sit in a big room all day, creating Excel spread-sheets. He also said we should enjoy the feeling of a breeze on our faces now, because in the future there will be so many plastic bags floating around in the atmosphere that breezes will no longer exist.

He was wearing his T-shirt with the jokey checklist that

said, *Cocaine. Heroin. Poutine.* There were three boxes next to the three words, but only the poutine box had a checkmark in it. I smiled at his shirt and frowned at his disturbing scenarios and thought about how it's hard not to feel angry at all the people like Jeanie and Stuart who are so selfishly bringing children into this doomed planet of ours.

Jeanie told me about this dream she had where she and Stuart were adrift in the middle of the ocean on a flimsy life raft with huge waves all around them. Then her contractions started and Stuart somehow fell over the side and drowned, but she wasn't too upset — big surprise, I thought — because there were experts monitoring her from the shore, so she knew that she and the baby were in good hands. I said, "What kind of experts?" And she said, "Just smart people, I don't know." As soon as she gave birth, a jet boat zoomed over and towed her to safety. She asked the waiting experts, *Why couldn't you have done that when I was in labour?* They told her, *We wanted to see how you'd handle it.*

It sounded like a nightmare to me, but Jeanie said this dream was very empowering. She also felt calmer because her horoscope earlier that day had told her that *The world is not out to get you, so stop being so dramatic.*

I could relate, because when I was a mother I used to get bent out of shape about every tiny thing. I was a lot more stressed out. So stressed out that one night, I left Greg and our baby at home and went to a bar and cuddled up to a guy who told me that my hair looked like Daryl Hannah's hair in *Blade Runner*. I said, "You think I have replicant hair?" He said, "Fucking right on you do." We did a bunch of shots and the bartender told me that I should feel lucky because I was drinking with their Regular of the Month. They didn't have a picture of him up or anything, but it was an honour just the same. I thought that was awesome and said how it's rare in this day and age when an ordinary person is celebrated. I said, "Where are the awards for Excellent Spouse and Parent, right? Oh, sure, you can go to the bakery at the Superstore and ask them to ice that on a cake for you. You can take the cake home and sit down with a fork and eat the whole goddamn thing and feel good about yourself until you allow your brain to ponder how many calories you just consumed."

When I got home, my family was asleep and the house was very quiet. I got my iPod and stuck my earbuds in and put on my Party Singles playlist, and after a while I threw up and went to bed.

Did I feel guilty? It's hard to say. Sure, my husband tells me I'm beautiful, but do I believe him? Would he marry a woman he found unattractive? I doubt it. But once the three of us were at the park and there was a dog there, and Greg said, "Look at the cute dog!" And I looked at it, and it was hideous. Its jaw was malformed, or something. So there's that.

Another time it was winter, and it was too cold to walk around outside so the three of us went to a large shopping centre so we could walk around inside.

Our child was not yet at the age where he knew enough to ask us to buy him things. He was happy to look at the animals in the pet store and make friends with the child-sized mannequins in the clothing stores and ride the escalator up and down over and over again. We bought him French fries and ice cream and he clapped his hands and said, "Ooooh!" He was appreciative and loving and rarely kicked up a fuss about anything.

In the pet store, a single hamster sat alone in one of the cages. There was a bright yellow sign on the cage that read, *$3.00 off. This hamster only!* Greg thought that was funny but I thought it was the opposite of funny. Our boy couldn't read yet so he just squeezed our hands and made cooing sounds at the discounted hamster, which seemed to soothe it. I wanted to buy the poor thing, but Greg said, "No way. No rodents."

When I was a little girl, I had four hamsters in a row. The first one's name was Peanut, and he lived to be almost three years old. I loved that hamster so much. He used to sit on my shoulder and fall asleep in my hands. I even trained him to climb the stairs. Then with Peanut II, I paid less attention. By the time I was onto the third and fourth ones, I was hardly ever changing their wood chips. They died of neglect. I still have nightmares about it. They're pleading with me in these squeaky voices to add a few pellets to their food bowl, or just for God's sake give them some water because they're so very, very thirsty, and I say, *Peanut II — or Chelsea, or Chelsea II — please forgive me!* But they never do. I wake up crying every time.

The night before the two of us set off on our pilgrimage, which was what we had started calling our gummy-candy trip in a zany but also sort of desperate way, a man stood on the grass in the park across from our house and watched us while we ate our dinner.

Greg noticed him first and said, "Whoa, look at that crazy dude!" Then I could tell he immediately regretted saying anything because I am a worrier, and Greg had plans to go out later that evening but after that I didn't want him to go. I didn't want him going out with his buddy and having a good time mixing up obscure classic cocktails. I became worried that the man was deciding if he would try to find a way into our home and kill us. Most likely he would wait until Greg left and then he'd know it was only me, and that's when he would kick down our door. Bad things like that happened all the time.

The man stood on one leg and then the other, like his feet were getting tired and he wanted to give them a break. But otherwise he didn't move.

I told Greg I would feel safer if he stayed home. He said, "How do we know we're ever safe?" I said, "I like to live under the illusion of safety, but now that illusion has been shattered."

The sun set and the clouds went pink and the man was still there. Greg looked at the clock and said, "But he hasn't done anything." I said, "Please don't go." He said, "Okay. But I'd really rather be making Brain Busters and Maiden's Prayers and Corpse Reviver No. 2's with Dave." I said, "Fine, then go." So he went.

Then I was all alone in our quiet house and I felt really bad. Every sound outside was a threatening sound. I really, really wished he had stayed. I wished I had been able to make him. My heart was pounding and I knew I wouldn't be able to sleep so I opened a bottle of wine and found an erotic thriller on Netflix that was recommended to me based on my previous choices.

After a while I paused it, and I turned off all the lights and looked outside, and there he was. I had the feeling that he might do something at any moment, but he didn't. He just kept standing there on the grass. I was sick to death of him just standing there. I wanted to open the window and scream at him, *Why don't you do something?* But I didn't.

After all that, the gummy treats were a letdown.

I got a lobster and Greg got a cowboy boot. Big deal. They were prepackaged because the little old woman was on vacation. We said, "But this is our vacation!" The cashier shrugged and rang in the next customer's merchandise.

Then we walked behind the house, which was neither little nor old but the explanation for that was they had to upsize to accommodate the overstock, as if that made sense, and we lined up to view the semi-famous and inexplicably German-sounding "KinderBush," and prepared for another letdown. Our impatient fellow sightseers tried to jostle us out of position, but it was our turn and we were taking it. We held hands and stood our ground, and then we saw them.

We pointed out the faces to each other as they appeared. There was one with curly hair. There was one with chubby cheeks. The one in the middle would smile his radiant smile until you begged for mercy. The one at the bottom would pretend to be a stegosaurus sometimes. Between those two branches was one who'd know what you were really like, but would love you anyway. The one that was just beginning to bud would squirm away whenever you tried to snuggle him. The one surrounded by all those thorns would grow up and go to school. That one would really appreciate your zucchini bread. The one near the top would steal your freedom and your sleep and your peace of mind.

Our favourite was the one near the bottom, who would gradually insinuate himself into your peer group. Whenever you got a babysitter and went out without him, everyone would say, *Hey, where's he at tonight?* They would like him more than they liked you. When he was old enough, he'd go out with you to the bars and buy rounds for all your friends and they would cheer and raise him up onto their shoulders and adopt him and take him home, and that would be the end of that.

When we were done looking, we shuffled along. We exited the viewing area through a pergola decorated with a few old pacifiers and some scuffed-up Lego blocks. The other tourists oohed and ahhed loudly behind us, but after we left the premises we decided that the whole experience had been overrated.

The travel writer had probably been paid a lot of money by the little old woman's publicity squad to say what he'd said. Superhuman strength? We doubted it. Who knows — maybe the roses had actually been doll heads spray-painted red, or something.

We hadn't eaten anything besides the candy so we stopped for French fries and ice cream before we got back onto the highway. The fries were sufficiently crispy and the ice cream had a reasonably silky mouthfeel, but we still couldn't shake our disappointment. This whole time we'd been waiting for something wonderful to happen, but nothing did.

We threw away our garbage and Greg said, "Shall we go?"

I said, "Wait a minute." I took a photo of the chip truck because I thought we might want to remember this someday. Then I deleted it, because who was I kidding.

We got in the car.

When the three of us used to take road trips together, Greg would drive and I would sit in the back seat with the little guy, to keep him entertained.

I read him stories, and it took us forever to get through each book because he asked "Why is that happening?" at the end of every page.

I pointed out clouds that looked like rocket ships or corn-cobs or alligators. He'd always claim that he couldn't see the shape at first, so I'd have to explain which part of the cloud was the nose cone or the kernels or the deadly snapping jaws, but by that time it would have drifted apart anyway.

We played I Spy but he never understood the rules. He always told me the thing he spied before I had a chance to guess it, which was frustrating.

Occasionally he would amuse himself, but not very often. He played hide and seek with his teddy bear once. He sat there in his car seat and put the toy under his blanket and closed his eyes and counted to ten. Then he said, "Ready or not, here I come." He opened his eyes and looked around like he'd forgotten where he'd put the bear. After doing that for a while, he finally glanced down at the lump under his blanket. He gasped, and smiled, and pulled the teddy bear out. He held it up and shouted, "I found you!"

After the chip truck, Greg and I were both sitting in the

front seats, like we always do now. The car was quiet. Greg was driving and I was tired.

There were trees on both sides of the road, just trees and not much else, nothing interesting to distract me. The sky was clear blue.

It would have been easy to close my eyes and sleep, if I'd really wanted to.

## ESCAPE TO THE ISLAND

SO THE PROBLEM WAS, Richard and I couldn't really handle the parenting thing anymore.

It wasn't as though our Joshua-John was a bad kid. Far from it. He was great. You couldn't have asked for a better kid. Sweet, polite, kind-hearted. When he was a baby, especially, no problem. Sure, there was all the stuff we had to do, changing diapers and giving him bottles and bathing him and all that. He was a good sleeper and didn't cry much. We mostly kept him in his crib or his swing or the Jolly Jumper or the stroller, which only minimally impeded our own activities, so no complaints there.

Then he started kindergarten and his brain just exploded. Suddenly he wanted to talk to us all the time. I'd pick him up from after-school daycare and as soon as we got in the door he'd be babbling on about his day, and Richard and I would be like, "Whoa, whoa, we just got home too and we need to unwind a bit, you know, before delving into any sort of conversation

here." The two of us have always gotten that about each other —
that a mental and emotional buffer is not only preferable but
necessary. Unfortunately, Joshua-John did not get it.

Still, we were amazed at the progress he was making. He
had friends. I really didn't think any of the other kids would
like him, since he could be such a know-it-all sometimes. But
life is full of surprises, and once our boy was in the system
he seemed to be getting along fine. I guess we'd done our jobs
pretty well, thank you very much.

It soon became clear, though, that he was going to keep
growing and learning and figuring things out, and asking more
and more questions that we'd have to find answers to. You can
only look up so many facts on the Internet before your child
starts to think that maybe you don't know anything. We had
to make up some of the answers ourselves, which used a size-
able chunk of energy that I will fully admit was in very short
supply those days. The dilemma became: if you don't keep some
of that energy for yourself — to funnel into your own creative
pursuits or simply to get through the day — how can you, in
such a depleted state, be expected to parent effectively? That's
a question I'd like an answer to. Because children really take it
out of you. Yes, okay, they give you love, but it comes at a cost.
What kind of a person puts a cost on love?

Here's the real issue, though. One day, while I was flipping
through a magazine and Joshua-John was peacefully making a
craft — and I knew that was something to be thankful for, that
he could entertain himself like that; give the kid a toilet-paper
tube and some string and he'd spend a good hour turning

them into a pet snake — I thought to myself, I wake up and you're here. Then you go to school and we get a break for a while, but then school finishes and daycare finishes and you come back home and you're here for at least a couple of hours until you fall asleep. And then you're still here, but at least I can sit on the couch with your father and watch something stupid on Netflix for an hour before I collapse. Then there you are again in the morning and we have to make you breakfast, get you dressed, and send you off to school. And that cycle was going to repeat, forever.

Television certainly helped. Joshua-John liked a lot of different shows, a really wide range, so that was good. But he'd get bored easily, his attention span wasn't the greatest, so eventually he would look up at me with his big, blue eyes and say, "Will you please play with me?" I mean, Jesus.

On top of all that, there was the never-ending worry about the future. There are a lot of problems in this world, and I feel grateful every day that Richard and I are probably not going to be around to see the worst of it. But it sucks for Joshua-John that he's going to inherit the Earth when every storm is an extreme weather event and all the drinkable water is privately owned, and he'll have to buy his water at the store, and maybe he'll be smart and buy it on sale but good luck with that because his parents certainly aren't coupon users. I know we should be; I know there are deals to be had; but I just can't bring myself to care. When the weekly flyers arrive, either his father or I will immediately dump them into the recycling bin — which, at least, is a step in the right direction.

When I go shopping, I just go. I don't even make a list. It's more fun that way, more spontaneous. When you're the parent of a small child, you get your kicks wherever you can find them. It's a dull, dull job. And the responsibility of it! It's a killer. And they were starting to really pile up on us, the expectations — both the ones we placed on ourselves (a low bar, admittedly) and the ones society was foisting upon us. And then all of a sudden his teachers were breathing down our necks — fill out these forms, tell us if he wants one slice or two for Pizza Day (two, obviously) — and it was all getting to be too much.

So one evening after we put Joshua-John to bed, Richard and I sat down and looked at our options, which were limited, let's face it, and at the end of our discussion and after some half-hearted sex that seemed like a good idea at the time but ultimately left us both feeling old and vulnerable, we decided we would get a nanny.

THE WOMAN WE FOUND seemed fine when we first hired her. Her résumé was good and all of her references checked out. She had a nice smile, a nice way about her.

Joshua-John loved her immediately, which was notable, because Joshua-John didn't like a lot of things.

I put a potato in front of him once. Set it down on his plastic plate that was shaped like a spaceship, which was the only plate he'd eat from. There was no rhyme or reason for that, of course. At least if he'd used it as a prop to fire up his imagination, to role-play being an astronaut and zooming to the moon,

I could've understood it. But there was zero interaction with the spaceship plate — he just needed the spaceship plate.

So I put the potato on it, and he looked at the ugly, brown tuber sitting there, and then he looked at me.

I said to him, "That's a potato, Joshua-John. That's what french fries are made of."

Because earlier, when I'd said we were having spaghetti for dinner, he had screamed that he only wanted french fries.

I was standing at the stove, poking at the pasta with a fork but feeling my eyeballs wander to the spot under the sink where I always keep a bag of spuds, and I thought to myself, *No, Joyce. You are not giving in. Not this time.*

First of all, I don't own a deep fryer. Second of all, I know it's technically possible to make french fries without a deep fryer, but the process is much more time consuming, and at the end of it, I knew with absolute certainty that if my homemade fries didn't look and feel and taste exactly like the ones they make at McDonald's, Joshua-John wouldn't go near them anyway. In a fit of desperation, I rummaged in the freezer to see if we had any McCain five-minute shoestrings, because sometimes he would deign to eat those, but we were all out.

I was feeling a little resentful, and yes, also a little angry, just right at that moment, because I was tired and I wanted my son to stop his whining and complaining and demanding and to calmly and cooperatively consume the meal I had prepared for us. So I thought, *Let him see where his precious* pommes frites *come from.*

He started to cry.

Then he picked up the potato and hurled it at me, and I said, "That's it. You are not going to the zoo tomorrow."

Which was a relief to me, really, because I've never liked the zoo.

What was I supposed to do? Just stand there and take it? I had to show Joshua-John that women can be tough in the face of adversity, and that a mother is not just some soft, nurturing lump without any needs of her own.

Richard wasn't there for the potato incident. He was at work.

So much for feminism, right?

I WENT TO UNIVERSITY in the nineties. Back then the whole girl-power thing was so huge that a guy would open a door for you, and then very hesitantly ask if his door-opening made you feel uncomfortable, because of course he was aware that you fully had the power to open the door for yourself, and he only wanted to be polite, but if his politeness was offensive in any way — if you felt, for example, that it was sending the message that you needed a man's help to enter or exit a building — then he would totally understand, and he could hold the handle at the top while you grasped it at the bottom, and in that way you could jointly accomplish the fair and non-discriminatory transfer of door-handle ownership, and then you could go your separate but equal ways, and smile at each other or not, but probably not, because sometimes when a man smiled at a woman it could mean something else, which could make people feel uncomfortable.

That's how Richard and I met.

Twenty years later, I had his baby, and now we might as well be living in the fifties.

Except on top of raising our child and doing all the housework, I get to haul my behind to a crappy office job every day. So whoever invented girl power can choke and die on her invigorating messages of equality, as far as I'm concerned.

WE CAN'T CONTROL THINGS. We think we can, but we can't.

As much as we like to tell everybody that we're satisfied with our lives the way they are, pronounce about the contentment that permeates our days, have conversations with other parents in the schoolyard about this or that aspect of our children's routine and pretend that we are somehow invested in those aspects — "Yes, I agree, the games they play in gym class sound pretty fun, and inventive" — don't we all yearn to be more than what we are, to prove to all our high-school frenemies and smug aunts that we will actually achieve the lofty goals we'd set for ourselves way back when? "Oh, really? Good for you. We can't all be winners at life but I'm sure you'll be the exception."

I do.

I don't know about Richard, but Richard has other things going for him. Richard is a man, and men have certain freedoms, and I for one am not advocating for the criminalization of those freedoms. Maybe just a reduction, but definitely not an outright embargo. In any case, Richard told me once that his biggest dreams had already been realized — to be a husband and a father. And I said, "Yes, fair enough, but did you want to be those things with us?" And he said, "Of course." But he said it fast, maybe too fast, so who even knows about him.

We can only truly know ourselves, that's the terrifying fact at the bottom of it. And I know I want to be a successful cartoonist.

I already have a character. She's an ambivalent mother named Trudy and she is, if I say so myself, hilarious. She works at an office job that she hates and she's married to a man she has no respect for, and she has a young daughter who is starting school and of course that presents all sorts of opportunities for comedy. She is also having an affair with the kindergarten gym teacher, and after the two of them finish their furtive coupling in seedy motels, they brainstorm fun physical activities for the children and amuse each other by concocting silly names for the games, such as Jungle Jimmies and Who Put the Coconuts in the Pony's Mouth? These are of course repeated at the dinner table in Trudy's home, when she and her clueless, cuckolded husband ask their daughter about her day.

I FIND RICHARD MORE attractive now than when we were in university. He's slightly more macho. He used to burn incense in his dorm room, and to this day the smell of sandalwood turns my stomach.

A few weeks after we started going out, he wove matching "loveship" bracelets for us out of multi-coloured twine. The minute he fastened mine around my wrist, it chafed, so I told him it was nice and all, and thanks, but I had to cut it off immediately. He said he respected my decision. He wore his until the dye faded and the strands weakened and eventually disintegrated on their own.

God, I used to despise him. His simpering. The way he'd ask me after every reverent caress, "Does that please you, Goddess?" His tabbouleh breath falling on me like an avalanche of male insecurity.

Those days are long gone.

Richard also used to have weirdly feminine curls that framed the admiring gaze he'd fix on me with eerie intensity. A few of the rugby players on our floor in residence called him "Poodle Baby" because of that hair, and whenever I heard them lob the nickname his way, any remnants of lust for him would drain out of me completely.

Now he shaves his head because he's going bald, so there are no more curls to squirm against my face and neck when we "make love." Even more of a relief, we've stopped "making love" altogether, because who has the time? If Richard's in the mood, I'll lube up and he'll get in and out, and then he'll fall asleep and I'll lie there staring at the shadow that always forms in the slanted corner of our ceiling, which looks like a witch's hat.

I still don't have orgasms, but that's my fault because it's my own responsibility to figure out what does the trick, and I find masturbation unnerving. All that furtive reckoning with a hand mirror, all that dedicated focus on oneself with "A Girl Like You" by Edwyn Collins on repeat. The sensations that build and build until you feel like you're standing on the edge of a cliff and you want to jump, you do, but you're afraid to fall because falling means death so you just keep standing there, until eventually you turn around and go back home and whip up a cheese casserole.

Still, there's the sneaking sense that we've lost something, as women. Exactly what, I couldn't tell you. But something.

THE NANNY'S NAME IS Felicia.

I knew a girl with the same name back in high school who was shaped like a cello and would go behind the portables with any boy who asked. A lot of them did, and then they'd tell everybody about it afterwards, and one day I heard that she got pregnant and had an abortion but it was all for the best because the fetus had too many kidneys, which was a shame.

But our Felicia was different. For instance, at our introductory meeting when Richard complimented her on the form-fitting dress she was wearing, she looked at me and said, "I got it at Marshalls. My friend works there and she lets me use her staff discount. If you're interested, I could hook you up."

With all her talk about shopping, my husband got turned right off and gave us a vacant stare and stood up and said he was going to make himself a sandwich, did anyone else want anything? And Felicia and I smiled at each other and said, pretty much in unison, "No, thanks."

Once he'd left the room and disappeared into the kitchen, I said, "'Felicia' sounds sort of Irish. Are you Irish?"

She said, "No, but everybody asks me that."

I said, "I've been told I have Finnish eyes, but I don't know what that means."

And she nodded, like maybe she knew what it meant, but it didn't matter.

Nothing mattered except for the two of us sitting there, discussing the bedtime routine of the child playing at our feet, whom I was about to leave in her care so I could go to a restaurant with his father and eat breadsticks and make observations such as, "Why do some breadsticks have sesame seeds on them and some don't? The ones without sesame seeds aren't even worth anybody's time," in lieu of an actual conversation.

We figured we should test her out before fully entrusting our son's well-being to this person we didn't really know. But everyone has to start somewhere, and when we came home and Joshua-John's door was closed and he was presumably sleeping soundly on the other side, we couldn't have been happier. Her rates were so good, and she seemed so responsible. She even washed up the dishes before we came home!

So we told Felicia she was hired, right there on the spot.

She started arriving bright and early every morning. We gave her a key so she could let herself in and get Joshua-John up, which allowed us to sleep in a bit and then get ready for our own days with minimal hassle.

She was great at her job and we were thrilled with our decision to hire her. She'd get Joshua-John all ready for school, walk him there, drop him off, and then after a few hours to herself, she'd pick him up at three o'clock. Then she'd entertain him until Richard and I got home. She'd also manage to cook us a wonderful meal and have it steaming on the table when we walked in the door. Nothing fancy, but always enjoyable, and wholesome. Just like her personality.

For the first few weeks, we'd thank her and send her on her way at that point. But then we started asking her to stay longer and longer. At first only for dinner, because she was so good at getting Joshua-John to eat all of his vegetables. Then we kept her on hand to assist with the story-reading and tucking-in portion of the evening. Eventually, we were paying her right up until our own bedtimes. Partly because she was so helpful, but mostly because she was just such pleasant company.

YOU KNOW HOW YOU think your life is going to go one way, but then it doesn't?

Before I met Richard, I had a very tumultuous relationship with a complete asshole who didn't give a shit about my feelings. I was sure I would marry him. We had this passion, this fire, that was extremely compelling at the time. I never knew where I stood with Darius, and that uncertainty kept me sizzling for him. We'd make plans to go on a date and he wouldn't show up and then he'd call me later that night, drunk, and tell me I was the only girl he'd ever loved, and did I want to come over and lick him up and down, and I'd say yes, yes, a thousand times yes. And then I'd show up at his dorm room and he'd be in there with somebody else, usually a woman who was much more attractive than I was, and he'd smirk and slap her ass and send her on her way, and open his arms for me and I'd fall into them like a rag doll.

I confided this to Felicia one night after Richard and I

returned home quite late from our first and only experience of indoor tandem skydiving, which was exhilarating, but also made us both throw up afterwards. She'd often encourage us to go on date nights, saying it was really no trouble at all, but we'd say we were just as happy to stay in. Then she started buying us gift certificates for things like the skydiving and couples massages and tango lessons and papier-mâché-heart-making workshops, which were of course impossible to refuse due to all the thought involved, but which made us feel hollow and anxious. Still, they were sweet gestures. And pricey! We gave her a raise at one point because we felt guilty she was spending such a big chunk of her earnings on us.

So we got in, and yawned and stretched and thanked Felicia again for the unique opportunity to hold hands in a wind tunnel, and she told us she'd had a lovely time playing trains with our son, and I wondered where she found the patience. Then Richard went up to bed, and I sat down next to her on the couch and asked if she'd ever been in love with a bad boy. And she said of course she had, wasn't that a rite of sexual passage for all young women?

She told me that in her early teens she used to frequent a particular mall food court because there was a security guard there who gave her the eye every time she sat down with her meatball sub or pizza bagel or chicken teriyaki. When buying her lunch got to be too expensive, she started bringing a packed one from home just so she could continue to sit at one of the plastic tables and feel the ridges of the security guard's utility belt as he brushed too close to her on his rounds. One day, he leaned over and murmured in her ear, "Come with me." She didn't really want to but part of her did, so she followed him to the back of the food court by the public restrooms. His key ring jangled as he unlocked a door she'd never noticed before, marked FOR SECURITY PERSONNEL ONLY, and that was when she lost her nerve. She backed away and shook her head, saying, "No, thank you, I've changed my mind." Then she swerved sideways and pushed through the door to the ladies' room, which was empty and she was briefly alone before the guard walked in too, snarling at her, "You think you can escape to your little island and I'm not going to follow you?" He pressed her up against the wall so the hand dryer was digging pain- fully into her back, and he held her wrists over her head with one hand and he shoved the other down the front of her jeans. Luckily, right then the door swung open and a group of chattering new moms with their tiny new babies strapped to their chests filed in. The man released Felicia, but his pres- ence was still obviously strange, and the moms stopped talking and scowled at him until he left.

"Which is why," Felicia said, patting my knee, "I am indebted to all mothers, no matter what they're like."

I was still in shock from her story, so I can't remember if I thanked her for that, or not.

SOMETIME LATER, FELICIA SAID she had a favour to ask.

We said, "Anything!"

The three of us were enjoying some wine and an assort- ment of cheeses, after Joshua-John had gone down, sitting comfortably together in the living room. *Almost like family members*, I remember thinking. But of course not exactly.

Felicia put down her glass and cleared her throat. She did everything delicately, but with purpose, so her throat-clearing sounded like a deliberate act, as if there was a morsel of pasta stuck in there from dinner, maybe, and she needed to dislodge it as well as broach the subject of taking our son trick-or-treating for Halloween.

"Oh," I said. "You want to do that?"

"I'd really, really like to, yes," said Felicia.

"Aren't we supposed to do that?" said Richard.

No one answered him, so I asked her, "What's he going to be, again?"

"A robot," she said.

"Oh, yes." I nodded. "I remember now."

Richard ate some cheese. "What does the costume look like?"

"I made it out of empty egg cartons," she told him.

"Ah," he said. "Is that why there are so many eggs in the fridge now, just sort of rolling around?"

"Exactly." She looked proud of him.

"What's the weather supposed to be like on Halloween?" I asked her.

"Clear, though a bit cold," she said. "But don't worry — I designed his robot suit so he could wear it over his coat."

"Clever," said Richard.

Her cheeks reddened a little. "Thank you."

He speared more cheese with a toothpick. "When is it, again?"

"Tomorrow night."

"Wow."

I knew what he meant. It's amazing how time flies when you're a parent.

The three of us sat there for a while, finishing up our wine.

"Well," I said, "I don't see the harm in it."

"Me neither," said Richard.

"Do you want to stay in with me and hand out candy to the neighbourhood children?" I asked him.

"Not really."

"Shall we go to a movie, then?"

"Sounds good."

Felicia stood up. "Thank you," she said, and gave us both affectionate glances before she left us for the night.

RICHARD AND I DIDN'T end up seeing a movie after all. He had to work late, and honestly I didn't even care because nothing good was playing.

I came home early because I was feeling lonely, and ate dinner with Felicia and Joshua-John. She made us a dish she called "Halloweenies and Beanies," which was baked beans with cut-up pieces of hot dog in it. It was surprisingly delicious.

After the meal, I asked Joshua-John if he would put on his costume for me, and he said, "It's Halloween, Mommy. I have to put it on."

And I said, "Of course."

He ran to his room and Felicia ran with him because, she said, she had to help him pull the straps over his shoulders, otherwise the whole thing would fall apart.

I sat in the living room with my hands in my lap. I felt like I was waiting for my prom date to arrive and take me to the dance, wondering if he'd bring me a corsage because that would prove that he really, truly loved me.

When Joshua-John emerged — Felicia making a poor but endearing attempt at a drumroll behind him, banging her hands on her thighs for added effect — I couldn't help myself. I stood up and clapped.

The costume itself was nothing special. It was just a bunch of empty egg cartons fastened together somehow — with tape? Glue? Staples? I couldn't tell how she'd done it, which was part of the magic — and spray-painted silver. An empty Kleenex box, also spray-painted silver, was fitted over the top of his head, with two vaguely frightening red eyes drawn on the front.

My son's face glowed with pride, his grin stretching all the way across. When I applauded, he took a stiff bow, then stuck out his arms and straightened his back and shuffled over to me. He got as close as the bulky outfit would allow, and sort of nuzzled his Kleenex box against my side and then peered up at me, and I saw Felicia had painted his little face silver too. The effect was unsettling because suddenly he seemed like he wasn't my child at all. Even though I could tell that under the makeup, yes, there were my boy's shining blue eyes and sweet snub nose, and there were his perfect, plump lips all puckered up like a fish gasping for air.

"I think he wants to give you a kiss," said Felicia. "Only it's hard for him, because he can't move very well."

"Ah," I said. "All right, then." So I bent over and gave him a peck. The greasy pigment that transferred to my own mouth made me wince, but I didn't wipe it off until Felicia had looped the handle of Joshua-John's trick-or-treat bag over his arm, led him to the foyer, helped him into his boots, and then told him to wave goodbye to me before she closed the door behind them.

AFTER THEY LEFT, I turned out all the lights because I'd been expecting to go to a movie with Richard and hadn't bought any candy to hand out.

I sat in our dark house and considered turning on the TV because I wanted to watch something, but the light of the screen might have given my presence away, and I didn't want the teenagers to be angry with me.

I sat on the couch and thought about what I wanted. *What do I want? What do I want?*

And then I knew.

I crept to our front window and slid it open slightly and pulled up the blind, but only a few inches. I had to hunch over awkwardly to peer out, but that was better than having my entire form outlined for potential hooligans to detect, and then punish.

The street was packed with children and their caregivers rushing up and down the sidewalks, zigzagging across garden paths, trampling over lawns. The air was full of happy shrieks and the rustling of bags as they filled up with candy, as well as various spooky sound effects being piped out of open doors: rattling chains, spine-chilling howls, anguished moans.

Adults huddled in laughing clumps, fond heads wagging. I didn't expect to see Felicia and Joshua-John because I figured they'd be long gone by now, up and around a corner somewhere, and I was right.

I counted twelve princesses, ten superheroes, six vampires, four butterflies, three tigers, and one adorable fried egg. There were too many skeletons and devils and ghosts to keep track of, so I didn't even try.

At one point, a rowdy gang of older kids smashed a pumpkin in the middle of the road and huddled around the guts. Then they jumped up and hurled wet, mushy handfuls at the row of cars parked in front of our house. Richard had our hatchback, so no problem there. Poor Felicia would have a big mess to clean off her windshield before she went home, though.

Then, with a sigh of relief, I realized that her little red sedan wasn't in its usual spot, and I thought, *Good for her.*

Because she was a good person, and she didn't deserve that.

# ACKNOWLEDGEMENTS

I'M VERY GRATEFUL FOR the financial support I received from the Ontario Arts Council through their Writers' Reserve program (many thanks to the publishers who recommended my work), and the Canada Council for the Arts through their Grants for Professional Writers program.

These stories, and my life in general, have been improved immensely by literary kindred spirits Shannon Alberta, Kelli Deeth, Sarah Henstra, and Grace O'Connell. I'm so grateful for their close, careful, and generous first readings of my work, and for their friendship.

A number of these stories began in workshops led by Sarah Selecky and Stuart Ross, and Joy Williams helped me develop "He Will Speak to Us" at the 2011 Tin House Summer Writers' Workshop. I'm grateful for their help, and for their fiction, which inspires and delights me.

Thank you to Neil Smith and Zsuzsi Gartner. I am a monster

fan of their writing, and the fact that they're fans of mine makes my heart explode.

Thank you to the Salonistas for wisdom, support, and friendship. And to the other communities of writers I've had the marvellous luck of finding. Where would we be without our fellow writers to buoy us up, confide in, and cheer us on? Someplace sad, I think.

Thank you to the librarians and the booksellers (most especially the independent ones) for the good and important work they do. And thank you so much to the readers (especially the ones who still read actual books on public transit).

Many thanks to the editors who previously published — and helped me to hone — some of these stories.

I've been dreaming of having Julia Breckenreid's art on my book cover since I first laid my eyes on her work. Thank you, Julia, for being awesome.

Thank you to the incomparable Derek Wuenschirs for so nicely rendering my photographic likeness.

An enormous thank you to Sam Hiyate and Kelvin Kong of The Rights Factory, whose continued faith in my writing, and tireless championing of it, mean the world to me.

I owe a whopping thank you to Marc Côté and Bryan Ibeas of Cormorant Books, whose ongoing enthusiasm for my fiction has been such a lifeline. Marc, your belief in my ability, and your guidance (both editorially and personally) and exhilerating insight, are dearly and deeply appreciated. Bryan, it's always a blast to work with you, and I was so thrilled to have your uncannily perceptive editorial input this time around. You're a gifted editor, and my stories are richer for your hand in them. Thanks go as well to Angel Guerra and Tannice Goddard for their beautiful design work, to Shannon Whibbs for her eagle-eyed copy edit, and to Barry Jowett for his fastidious proofread.

Much love and many thanks to my friends and family for their love and encouragement, especially my parents Tim and Linda Westhead, my brother Cameron Westhead and his wife Marcella Campbell, the Wuenschirs family, Cousins Don and Kate and Laura, (Great) Aunt Lori, and my amazing Grandma Marion Westhead, who will be 102 years old when this book is published.

And to Derek and Luisa, my two favourites. Thank you for giving me the space I need to be spacey when I'm writing. Sometimes I get stuck in a story and the rest of life goes out the window because I just can't be bothered with it, and that glorious state of being wouldn't be possible without your love and support. And then I get to come home to both of you, my two fellow adventurers, and that is the best. I love you more than anything.

Photo: Derek Wuenschirs

# ABOUT THE AUTHOR

JESSICA WESTHEAD'S FICTION HAS been shortlisted for the CBC Literary Awards, selected for the Journey Prize anthology, and nominated for a National Magazine Award. Her stories have appeared in major literary journals in Canada, the U.S., and the U.K., including *Hazlitt*, *The New Quarterly*, *Maisonneuve*, *Indiana Review*, and Hamish Hamilton's *Five Dials*. Her first novel *Pulpy & Midge* was nominated for the ReLit Award. Her critically acclaimed short story collection *And Also Sharks* was a *Globe and Mail* Top 100 Book and a finalist for the Danuta Gleed Short Fiction Prize.

Earlier versions of the following stories were published previously:

"Not Being Shy" in *Five Dials*

"The Lesson" in *Found Press Quarterly*

"Baby Can't You See?" in *THIS Magazine*

"A Little Story About Love" in *Eat It: Sex, Food & Women's Writing* by Feathertale Press and in the online magazine *Don't Talk to Me About Love*

"Real Life" in *Room Magazine*

"Gazebo Times" in *Event Magazine*

"Dumpling Night" and "Empathize or Die" in *Taddle Creek*

"Things Not to Do" in *PRISM Magazine* (this story was inspired a piece I wrote for *The Litter I See Project*, created by Carin Makuz in support of literacy and Frontier College)

"He Will Speak to Us" in *Maisonneuve*

"Everyone Here Is So Friendly" in *The Puritan and in iLit — Reality Imagined: Stories of Identity and Change* by McGraw-Hill Ryerson Ltd.

"At Kimberly's Party" and "Puppybird" in *The New Quarterly*

"Prize" in *Hazlitt*

"Flamingo" in *The 2015 Short Story Advent Calendar*